MORE THAN A
Tiara

VALERIE COMER

ACKNOWLEDGMENTS

Thanks to my friend Angela Breidenbach, Mrs. Montana 2009, for her patience in coaching me through the ways of the pageant world. Any inaccuracies in *More Than a Tiara* are mine, not hers. I've learned so much working with her. I can't thank her enough.

Thank you to my husband, my kids, their spouses, and my grandgirls for not thinking I was crazy for writing a pageant-themed story. Or if they thought it, they didn't say it aloud. In my hearing, at least.

Much appreciation goes to Nicole for her encouragement, support, and editing. I couldn't have done this without her.

All my love to Jesus, the author and finisher of my faith, who cherishes me as the diamond central to His tiara... and He feels the same about you!

Valerie Comer Bibliography

Urban Farm Fresh Romance

0. Promise of Peppermint (ebook only)
1. Secrets of Sunbeams
2. Butterflies on Breezes
3. Memories of Mist
4. Wishes on Wildflowers
5. Flavors of Forever
6. Raindrops on Radishes
7. Dancing at Daybreak
8. Glimpses of Gossamer
9. Lavished with Lavender
10. Cadence of Cranberries
11. Joys of Juniper
12. Together in Thyme

Pot of Gold Geocaching Romance

1. Topaz Treasure
2. Ruby Radiance
3. Sapphire Sentiments
4. Amethyst Attraction

Miss Snowflake Pageant

1. More Than a Tiara
2. Other Than a Halo
3. Better Than a Crown

Farm Fresh Romance

1. Raspberries and Vinegar
2. Wild Mint Tea
3. Sweetened with Honey
4. Dandelions for Dinner
5. Plum Upside Down
6. Berry on Top

Cavanagh Cowboys Romance
(Montana Ranches Christian Romance)

1. Marry Me for Real, Cowboy'
2. Give Me Another Chance, Cowboy
3. Let Me Off Easy, Cowboy

Saddle Springs Romance
(Montana Ranches Christian Romance)

1. The Cowboy's Christmas Reunion
2. The Cowboy's Mixed-Up Matchmaker
3. The Cowboy's Romantic Dreamer
4. The Cowboy's Convenient Marriage
5. The Cowboy's Belated Discovery
6. The Cowboy's Reluctant Bride

Garden Grown Romance
(Arcadia Valley Romance)

1. Sown in Love (ebook only)
2. Sprouts of Love
3. Rooted in Love
4. Harvest of Love

Riverbend Romance Novellas

1. Secretly Yours
2. Pinky Promise
3. Sweet Serenade
4. Team Bride
5. Merry Kisses

valeriecomer.com/books

To my beloved husband, Jim,
who has treated me like a beauty queen
for well over thirty years.

I love you!

CHAPTER 1

*J*ust ahead of her, a group of at least a dozen people drifted into The Parrot Confectionery, talking and laughing. Marisa Hiller growled in frustration. First a large delivery truck blocked the alley so she couldn't drop her box of fresh rosemary at the back door, and now the front of the candy shop was clogged with customers. That's what she got for agreeing to Brian's late-afternoon request for the herb.

She shifted the large box to her other hip and peered in the wide windows. Yep. It would be a few minutes before she could edge her way through to the back of the business.

Her gaze caught on the wooden notice board nestled beside the door with dozens of posters in various degrees of tatter. Homemade ads with photos offered puppies, while tear-off strips provided the kennel's phone number. Pampered Chef parties, the Helena Symphony, a new daycare in town. People could live their whole lives off a board like this.

A larger poster in the top corner begged attention. Miss

Snowflake Pageant? She narrowed her gaze and stepped closer to see the details. Back in the day, she'd have been the first in line to sign up for that kind of competition. Now? Not so much. Not after...

"Marisa? Marisa Hiller?"

Had she slipped back in time? Was her memory playing tricks on her? But no. The voice had been real. She pivoted.

Jase Mackie.

Her gut lurched. What was he doing in Montana? She hadn't seen him since that day at the JFK airport. Since...

For a second he looked like the old Jase. The shock of red hair she'd once run her hands through. The blue-green eyes that once looked adoringly into her own. She'd kissed those freckles on his nose.

But then his eyebrows pulled together, and his gaze grew wary. "It is you. I thought I must have been imagining things."

"Real and in the flesh." Marisa did her best to tamp any feelings out of her voice. It'd been twenty-seven months and four days since they'd flung hostile words at each other beside the luggage carousel. She'd grabbed her bags and run for a taxi, blocking out not only Jase's words but Terry's. Yeah, that had gotten her fired. She was supposed to keep personal matters out of her work.

She yanked her gaze free of Jase's and glanced through the confectionery door beside her. Maybe she could squeeze past the late-season tourists peering into the candy case if she lifted the box above her head. "Been nice seeing you." *Liar.*

"You look good."

In jeans with a ripped knee? A tank top with tomato

stains? Not precisely the runway model apparel he'd last seen on her. Marisa's gaze snapped back to his.

He looked surprised to have let the words out then his chin jerked toward the notice behind her. "Going to enter that pageant? It looks right up your alley."

"I just noticed the poster, so I don't exactly have any plans. Never heard of it before." Not in this century, anyway.

"Oh." His gaze slid away, then back.

She'd missed him. Missed everything she'd dreamed might happen in those heady days.

Before he'd ruined everything.

Marisa took a deep breath. He'd never come after her. Never apologized. Her conscience pricked. Not that she'd left a forwarding address with Terry. No, she'd left everything behind in one go. She'd returned to the apartment she'd shared with two Broadway actresses, packed up her stuff, rented a truck, and driven across the country. Mom needed her, she'd told herself. It'd been true. Still was. The farm wasn't huge, but it was theirs, and needed them both to make it work.

She shoved her hands into her jeans pockets. Jase didn't remember her with cropped, unpolished fingernails.

"Marisa, I—"

She shook her head, backing up a step. "I've got to go."

Jase reached past her and tapped the poster.

Every fiber of her being stretched toward the heat from his arm. She shifted away. If only she could move nearer instead.

"You should consider entering. I can totally see you doing something like that."

3

She blew out a breath. The nerve. "You lost any chance to give me advice."

"It's not advice." A shadow crossed his face, and his lips tightened. "I'm a friend drawing attention to something you may not have noticed."

"You lost the right to call me your friend, too. What are you doing here, anyway? Go back to New York. Just get out of my life and stay there."

"This is home."

"Since when?" East-coast city boy, born and bred. Helena, Montana, might not be the Wild West anymore, but it wasn't big enough to hold the likes of Jase Mackie.

"My folks bought a resort west of town last year, planning to semi-retire, and I moved my studio here a few months ago." He pointed up the walking mall that'd been created along historic Last Chance Gulch.

She could make a snide comment about following Mommy and Daddy, but who was she to call the kettle black? She slept in her old bed, with her mother's room down the hall.

"How about you?"

Marisa lifted a shoulder. "This is where I grew up. On a farm."

His face brightened. "I'd love to do a piece on a local farm. Could I—?"

Their eyes collided for an instant, then the light went out of his and his shoulders slumped. "Never mind."

"I'd rather not." It would never do to be seen as eager. She wasn't. Not really. She'd been doing her best to forget him. Seeing him again created a pothole in her road, but she'd get back up to speed in a minute. But — what if he still cared? What if he was so awkward about their encounter for the same reasons she was? Attracted but burned. Oh man. Had she just admitted her infatuation, even to herself? Was there any hope?

She took a step back. "If you want to do a farmer story, get in touch with the Tomah CSA. There are more than a dozen member farms. Maybe someone will be happy to work with you."

"CSA?"

"Community supported agriculture. People in the Helena area can pay a monthly subscription fee and get a box of produce delivered every week."

"Oh. I've heard of that sort of thing."

Well good for him. It was her life. Her chosen life, she reminded herself. A worthy calling providing real food to people. She'd been trying to do that in Kenya, too.

Stay clear of Jase Mackie. He's a dream smasher.

She pivoted and yanked the door to The Parrot open. She'd edge her way to the back one way or another.

"Marisa!"

She'd walked away in JFK, and she could do it again.

JASE PULLED into the parking lot at Grizzly Gulch Resort. He rested his forehead against the Jetta's steering wheel. Man, he'd bungled that. For over two years he dreamed of what he'd say, how he'd apologize — if he ever found her again. How she'd throw herself in his arms and forgive him for being an idiot.

Um, right. Hadn't happened. But still, he'd seen her. She

looked as good as always, even with minimal makeup and her long brown hair pulled back into a lopsided ponytail. The casual look of someone who worked for a living and got her hands dirty, like that day in Kenya.

He'd been over her forever already, hadn't he? After all, he'd been seeing Avalon for several months. Did Avalon even have a down-to-earth side?

She definitely couldn't hold a candle to Marisa.

He groaned and thumped his head on the wheel a couple more times for good measure. Maybe he'd knock some sense into himself.

A tap sounded on the car window. "Jase?"

He glanced up at his sister's concerned face. With a sigh he pulled the handle and opened the car door.

Kristen stepped out of the way as he pulled himself out. "You okay, little brother? You look like you just had a nightmare."

"I'm fine."

"You don't look it."

"Thanks. I think." He glanced around the parking lot and spotted her rental car. "I didn't know you were coming up this weekend. Did you bring the kids?"

"Yes, they're around back in the playground with Dad. Todd had to work, and you know how much the kids love it here. So much more room to go wild than our apartment."

Jase fell into step beside her as they headed toward the side door that led to their parents' penthouse suite. "Why did you come?"

She turned laughing eyes and pouting lips his way. "At least pretend you're happy to see me." Her elbow caught his side.

"Why wouldn't I be? You're my favorite sister."

"The only one." Kristen sighed dramatically. "Good thing I gave you a niece and nephew, or you wouldn't even notice my existence."

"Not so." He grinned down at her. "But it does help."

"You need to get married and have a family, Jase. Seriously. The kids adore you. And besides, they need cousins. You wait too much longer, and Charlotte will be old enough to babysit instead of play with them."

Images of Marisa flooded his mind. She wore a strappy gown and crazy tall heels like on the runway in Milan, shorts and beachwear as she had in Kenya, jeans—

"Earth to Jase?" Kristen's voice mocked his thoughts. "Your brain headed over to — what's her name — Avalon, isn't it? When do I get to meet her and see if she's worthy of my little brother?"

He gave his head a quick shake. "Oh, she won't be." In his mind, Avalon frowned, her lips pulling into a pout as though tempting him to kiss her displeasure away. But it was true. Kristen would see through Avalon in a heartbeat. Why hadn't he? Why had it taken a chance encounter with—?

"Right." Kristen studied him as he reached past her to open the door to their parents' penthouse suite. "Well, I can solve your problem."

"My problem?" A wave of irritation sloshed over him. "It's none of your business, sweet sister."

Kristen went on as if he hadn't interrupted. "The pageant is drawing in all these beautiful, poised women. You might meet somebody new."

Or someone from his past.

7

"Hi, you two." Mom floated over. "Dinner's ready, so you're just in time. Grandpa will be up in a minute with Charlotte and Liam."

"Sounds good." Kristen dropped her briefcase on the marble kitchen island. "Guess what I found out." She opened the latches and pulled out her laptop.

Jase leaned his elbows on the counter and faked a bright, interested smile. "The sun sets in the west?"

"Oh, you." She swatted at him, and he shied away with years of practice. "No, really. Mom and I were talking last weekend about how registrations for the pageant have been kind of slow."

He'd been in Wyoming, shooting a fall wedding on a leaf-studded ranch. "There's still lots of time."

"Yes and no. The businessmen are loath to sink their money into it if we don't get a big name or two on the list. Somebody who will pull in some attention for the pageant among all the other events going on for Helena's 150th birthday. We may not need a full docket for another month, but we do need the right woman or two to make sure people take the event seriously."

Hmm. That made some kind of sense.

"And I found someone. I mean, not that I've asked her yet, but it's why I'm here this weekend." Kristen's green eyes glowed with excitement.

The door flung open and a four-year-old locomotive slammed into Jase's leg. "Unca Jase! Unca Jase! I comed to see you!"

Jase squatted and pulled his nephew into a hug. "Hey, Liam. Good to see you, buddy." He reached out his other hand, and Charlotte placed hers in it with a little curtsy. "Princess Charlotte." He pressed a kiss on her palm. He knew how mere subjects presented themselves to royalty.

"Sir Uncle Jase, I am pleased to see you." Then the princess dissolved into little-girl giggles and snuggled against him.

"See? Jase needs kids of his own."

He looked up at his sister, whose hands waved as she talked to their parents. Sure, he wanted a family, but at the right time. With the right woman. He blocked Marisa's image and plunked on the floor to tickle the stuffing out of these two.

"It wasn't as difficult as I thought," Kristen went on. "There weren't many descendants along the way, but you'll never guess what I found."

All tickling aside for the moment, Jase leaned against the base of the leather love seat. "What are you talking about, Kris? I'm completely lost."

"Oh. Mom and I talked about how cool it would be if we could find a descendant of Calista, the first pageant winner in 1889, the year Montana became a state. If there happened to be a woman of suitable age, etc, and she could be persuaded to run, we'd easily get all the backers we need for the whole pageant."

"Sounds like a long shot."

Liam tackled him again, stubby fingers inflicting more pain than pleasure.

"It seemed like it." Kristen nodded. "But it turned out to be a fabulous idea. There is one person who has the perfect credentials, more than we'd dreamed of."

"Tell us already."

So Mom found Kristen's penchant for dramatic effect as annoying as Jase did.

"Okay. So you know Calista married Albert, who'd been the owner of the original Tomah Inn. The family sold it in the thirties and bought a small farm on the other side of Helena. And they still live on that farm."

"It would help if Miss Snowflake is a local girl." Mom sounded excited, even though she wasn't so local herself.

"Right. But it's even better than that."

The laptop creaked open, but Jase couldn't see the screen from his spot on the floor.

"She's actually modeled in New York. She's drop-dead gorgeous. See? She's done a bunch of work for Juicy Couture. Tory Burch. Michael Kors." Kristen glanced over at Jase. "You might even know her. You've shot sessions for some of those designers, haven't you?"

Jase's jaw clenched and the room tilted a little. Good thing he was already on the floor. He held Liam off at arm's length. "What's her name?" But he knew.

CHAPTER 2

*C*haos whirled around Marisa as women loaded tomatoes, peppers, and a host of other vegetables into various car trunks. Nearly a dozen dirt-smudged children dodged in and out as they played tag, barely averting mishap. Baxter, Mom's old collie, bounded between them, clearly delighting in the game.

Marisa wedged two red kuri squashes on the floorboards beneath a toddler's car seat. The vehicle wouldn't hold much more, but the tyke loved squash while refusing most other vegetables.

She'd grown to love all these little ones. Heading toward thirty herself with no diamond dangling in front of her, she might never have kids of her own. Not that the young moms chattering behind her had diamonds — or husbands, either, for that matter. They'd made strings of bad decisions, but they were trying. Besides, it wasn't the kids' fault. They still deserved healthy food and a bright future. She could help with both.

The first carload chugged down the driveway. A late-model white sedan sat at the mailbox, signal light on, as the young mom steered her clunker around it.

Marisa cocked her head and narrowed her eyes. Not a car she recognized. It couldn't be Jase's, could it? Why would he track her down in 24 hours when he hadn't in 27 months? Anyway, the driver's silhouette wasn't tall enough.

She sighed and turned on the hose at the greenhouse. Might as well rinse the worst of the dirt off her hands before shaking the hand of someone she didn't know.

The car — a rental from Avis — purred to a stop beside her and a woman got out, reddish hair swinging to her shoulders. Pretty smile directed her way. "Marisa Hiller, by any chance?"

"Yes, that's me. Have we met?"

The woman hesitated. "I don't think so. I'm Kristen O'Brien, partly from Salt Lake City."

And partly from Beverly Hills?

Marisa shoved the thought aside and wiped her hands dry on dirt-smudged jeans. She held one out to Kristen. "Pleased to meet you."

When Kristen smiled, freckles danced on her nose. She shook Marisa's hand. "Likewise." She gestured toward the turmoil as the two remaining young women corralled children into vehicles. "I wanted to speak with you, but it seems I should have called ahead to make an appointment."

"Marisa! Did you say you found more canning jars?" Bren Haddock called out from beside her battered car.

"A moment, please," Marisa said to Kristen as she turned to Bren. "Yes, Mrs. Abercrombie donated dozens of them last week when she moved into the condo. They're mostly quarts. How many do you need?"

Bren eyed the hatchback full of boxes of ripe tomatoes. "We figured this was about a hundred pounds? So four dozen, if you've got that many."

Thankfully, she did. Ever since the women's group at church had clued into Marisa's ministry, they'd scoured their cellars and neighborhoods for unused jars and tools. Mrs. Abercrombie had even donated all the proceeds from the garage sale she'd held before her move, enabling Marisa to buy a tool shed to put on the five acres she'd set aside for her families to use.

"Excuse me," Marisa said to Kristen. "The gang is nearly ready to head home, and I have a few things to do. In ten minutes, it will all be quiet."

"Sure. Thank you." Kristen glanced toward the greenhouse. "Mind if I look around a little? I promise not to touch anything or snoop."

Marisa had nothing to hide. She shrugged. "Go for it." She turned to Bren. "Let's find you some jars. Do you even have room for them?"

"In the front seat." She peered into the hatchback. "You kids stay buckled up, you hear? I'll be back in a minute."

Marisa passed boxes of jars out to Bren then tossed a few packages of snap lids into the last one. Courtesy of the women's group.

Bren stuffed the last box into the hatchback and turned to Marisa, surprising her with an impulsive hug. "Thanks so much. You can't begin to understand how much you've done for my kids."

Marisa hugged her back. "It's not me. You're doing all the work. I'm just giving you a place to do it."

"And friends. And support. I couldn't do it without you."

"You're a good mom. You'd have found a way, but I'm so thankful God brought us together."

A shriek billowed out the car's open windows. "Mommy, make him stop!"

Marisa grinned and peered in. "Hey, buddy. Quit picking on your sister. Are you going to help your mom can tomatoes tonight?"

Eight-year-old Davy shook his head emphatically. "No, I'm going to eat them. With salt and pepper."

"All of them?" Marisa's eyebrows rose.

The boy glanced over the back seat. "Not all of them today."

Bren started the car, and the exhaust backfired. The engine didn't sound so good either. But what more could Marisa do? She didn't know a mechanic who'd be willing to donate time. She waved as the heavily loaded car rumbled down the driveway then turned back to the greenhouse to finish cleaning up for the day.

Oops. The white sedan. The red-haired woman.

Thankfully Mom had noticed her oversight. She and Kristen strolled toward the house, chatting and laughing like old friends, with Baxter beside them. Marisa lengthened her stride and caught up just as Mom pointed Kristen to a wicker chair on the porch.

"There you are, Marisa! Did Kristen tell you why she came to the farm?" Mom held the kitchen's screen door open.

"No, she didn't have a chance yet. Do you want me to pour some lemonade?"

"I'll get it. You've been working hard. Just sit down and visit with our new friend." Mom disappeared and the screen door smacked shut.

Kristen dropped into the wicker chair. "I was just telling your mom that I'm very interested in your family history."

"Oh?" Some kind of long-lost cousin, perhaps? Unlikely. The clan had never run to large families. Marisa settled onto the porch swing and let it twist.

"Yes. My parents bought a resort here last year. I understand your ancestors owned it back when it was still known as the Tomah Inn."

Also until her ancestors' lives had soured in the Great Depression. At least they'd been able to sell it for enough to buy this farm. She'd rather have thirty acres of farmland than a swanky inn any day of the year.

Mom brought out a tray with a plate of cookies and three glasses of lemonade, clinking with ice cubes, and set them on a side table. "It's good to see something happening there again. It's changed hands so many times and fallen into neglect."

"Yes. It was so well constructed back then the rose rock exterior of the original building suffered little from the neglect. The interior — well..." Kristen laughed. "It needed a lot more work to bring it up-to-date while keeping the charm. All new electrical and plumbing, of course, with everything else restored as much as possible. You should come see it. It's a piece of Helena's history. Your family's history."

Marisa reached for a lemonade. "Maybe sometime. The farm is very busy this time of year. Frankly, we almost welcome the first heavy frost of the fall so the craziness subsides."

Kristen turned sparkling green eyes on Marisa. "That is so fascinating. I've never been on a farm before. I do grow herbs on my kitchen windowsill. Does that count?"

It would take a mighty large windowsill to supply The Parrot with enough rosemary for their salted caramels. "It's a great start." Why did Kristen care? Maybe it didn't matter. Marisa couldn't help liking her anyway.

"We have a bit of memorabilia from the family's early days at the inn. Why don't I show you?" Mom hurried into the house and came back a moment later with a carved wooden box.

Tucking a strand of long hair behind her ear, Kristen leaned over as Mom opened it. "Oh, how interesting. Like what?"

Mom set a newspaper clipping on the table along with a few photographs. "My great-great-grandmother was the first winner of the Miss Snowflake Pageant. But she didn't keep the tiara. She'd also won a bigger prize."

Kristen glanced at Marisa.

Awareness settled over Marisa like a suffocating blanket. So that's why the visitor was here. She could see it clearly now. She surged to her feet, and the swing slammed the back of her knees. "No."

Creases furrowed Mom's forehead as she glanced up. "No, what?"

"No, I'm not entering. That part of my life is over."

Mom looked from one to the other. "Who said anything about—"

Marisa locked eyes with Kristen. "If you're here to

dredge up old history and ask me to enter the pageant, the answer is no."

"They're bringing back the pageant?" Mom's voice rose as excitement caught hold. "But, Marisa—"

"Mom, don't even start."

"My brother said you'd say no."

Marisa's eyes narrowed. "Your brother?"

"Jase. He said it was a waste of my time to talk to you, but I had to try. It means so much to the community."

"Jase. You mean—" Marisa took a deep breath and closed her eyes. The red-gold hair. The sparkling smile. Eyes as green as a glacier-fed lake. Of course she was Jase's sister.

"Is that *the* Jase I heard so much about?" Mom was clearly lost.

She wasn't the only one. *Focus, Marisa.* "The community? You said you live in Salt Lake City."

"I do, but this is my parents' home and my brother's. I'm an event planner, so Dad and some of the other hotel owners asked me to run the pageant to coincide with Helena's 150-year anniversary. There are so many events going on we're having a bit of trouble lining up enough sponsors. The business community is holding back, not fully investing in the idea until they believe it will be a success. They haven't caught the vision of how many visitors a pageant like this could bring to the city this fall. Besides, it's a special birthday for the state of Montana, too."

"It's a wonderful idea." Mom clasped her hands together. "You would do Calista proud, my dear. Maybe history would re—"

"I said no." Marisa cast an apologetic glance at Kristen.

"It's not that I want the pageant to fail or tourism to struggle or that I don't care about my city or my state, but I'm busy here. You saw the families leaving as you drove in. These are people I can make a difference for. They are whom my life revolves around."

Kristen's gaze softened. "The economy has been so hard on them, hasn't it?"

Marisa crossed her arms. The woman with all those glittering rings on her fingers had no idea. "It has."

"Don't you see? This pageant can make a real difference. Bringing tourists in strengthens everything. It provides more jobs, so parents can take better care of their families." Kristen's gesture took in the vegetable gardens lining the driveway. "They need so much more than food."

"Grandmother Calista cared for those in need, too. That's why she entered the pageant back in her day." Mom pulled a sheet of music out of the wooden box. "That's why she chose *Away in a Manger* for her talent piece. She knew poor children were lucky to have even a stable to sleep in, let alone enough to eat, and she believed she could help."

"I'm already making a difference." Even if Jase didn't think so, or approve. Jase. Had he sent his sister here?

"Every contestant nowadays competes with a platform." Kristen smoothed the front of her skirt. "Some support a cure for diabetes or heart disease or autism. There are many worthy causes." She looked up and faced Marisa squarely. "But there are never too many voices for the poor, the marginalized. The pageant could multiply what you can do on your own."

Marisa rubbed her hand across her forehead, where a

headache threatened to set in. "This doesn't sound like the Jase I used to know. What's in it for him?"

"My brother? He's the official event photographer."

Enter the pageant and give him room to criticize her again? No. "Even more reason not to change my answer."

CHAPTER 3

*O*h, no, that looks like a blemish." Avalon Penhaven leaned over Jase's shoulder and peered at herself on the computer screen. "Zoom in on the left cheek, high up. See that?"

Jase gritted his teeth and tapped the stylus on the area she'd indicated. He'd already zoomed Photoshop in so far no one could tell whose face he touched up.

"Jase, darling, you have to fix it before Dad sees it."

His nose twitched at her floral scent. He barely had time to turn his face away before he sneezed. "Excuse me." He reached for a tissue from the box on his desk.

At least Avalon stepped back. "Are you coming down with something? I haven't had my flu shot yet. I hope I don't get sick."

"No, I'm fine." At least he would be if she gave him a little space. He tapped the screen again to zoom out.

Avalon Penhaven in front of him, Avalon Penhaven behind him. Two Avalons too many. What had he seen in her, anyway? He studied her virtual face.

"I thought you would fix that spot and even out my complexion."

"If I evened out your complexion any more than this, you'd be left looking like an unbaked pastry. Your face needs its natural tones." He tipped his head and examined the image critically. "Besides, at this resolution, I can't even pick out the bit you were talking about."

"Oh, Jase, don't be silly. I just want to look my best for Mother and Dad."

He pushed the rolling chair back and swiveled so he could see the real Avalon, not the princess in the computer.

She backed up a step and perched on the edge of the upholstered visitor's chair a few feet away, twisting both hands around a pair of knit striped gloves.

"Why are you so worried, Avalon? Your parents love you. And besides, you're one of the most beautiful women I've ever met." It was no more than the truth, and he'd made a living taking photos of drop-dead gorgeous women.

Avalon's head jerked up and she met his gaze. "Really? Do you think so?"

Jase tried not to pull his eyebrows together in a frown, but it was difficult. How could she not know? "Really."

"But..."

He reached for her hand, and she clung to him with amazing ferocity. "And you have more going for you than beauty. You have your degree in investment. You get great acting roles with Grandstreet Theatre." She ought to. For Avalon, everything was staged.

"Dad wanted a boy."

And he'd taken it out on his daughter?

She looked down again, her Sergio Rossi boot tracing

the wood grain of his studio's floor. "It's hard to be good enough when your parents wanted something else completely."

A trickle of sympathy niggled against his better judgment. His parents had encouraged him and Kristen to find themselves and be the best they could be, but not so they'd look good in front of their parents' friends. Happiness was their goal. That, and following God's call on their lives. "No one can be good enough on their own. The only one we actually need to worry about impressing is God, and it's not possible without His help."

She jerked her hand away. "Don't be ridiculous. I've decided to enter the Miss Snowflake Pageant, so I need that portrait perfect for my portfolio."

Jase turned back to the computer and examined the fictitious Avalon one more time. Her long hair, streaked blond, swung past her shoulders. He'd managed to catch a sparkle in her brown eyes that didn't always exist. A face perfectly made up. Having looked away for a minute, he couldn't begin to guess where she'd wanted a touch-up.

He clicked save. "I'll get the flash drive to you tomorrow."

"Jase? Do you think I'll win?"

He turned back to face her, making certain a casual grin was in place. "I'm not a judge, just the event photographer. A pageant can get quite grueling, but I'm sure you're up for it. You'll do fine."

"You don't understand."

"Don't do it for your father. Do it if you want to, for yourself and whatever cause you choose to promote."

"Cause?" Her eyes flared in alarm.

Yeah, he'd seen that coming. "The contestants each have a platform they promote. It can be nearly anything that means a lot to you."

"Like what?"

He shrugged. "Some women bring awareness to social conditions. Others raise money for cancer research." His mind slid to Marisa. Would she join? "Some for hungry kids in Africa. I can't pick it for you. Just find something to be passionate about." *Besides yourself.*

She puckered her pretty face into a frown. "That sounds hard."

"You'll think of something." The timer jingled on his iPhone, and he pushed to his feet. "Sorry, I have another appointment arriving in five minutes."

Avalon rose, too, and leaned in to kiss his cheek. "Thanks, Jase. I'll come by tomorrow for my photos. What time is good?"

"Any time after three." He wished he felt something besides sympathy as she strode for the door.

MARISA HEAVED a carton of eggplant off the tailgate of her truck.

"Let me get that." Bob Delaney reached for the box. "Any more where those came from?"

"Two more." She pulled off her work gloves and tightened her ponytail.

Bob eyed her. "You missed last night's CSA meeting."

She shot him a rueful grin. "Too busy. So much is still coming off the garden and with our hired help at part time now that school's in, it leaves more for me to do. Sorry I couldn't make it."

"We did have enough members there for a quorum." He plunked the box on the receiving table and turned back to her. "We made a decision or two we thought you should know about."

"Me?" It wasn't the first meeting of Tomah Community Supported Agriculture she'd missed. She'd get the minutes in her email and glance through them when she had time. December, perhaps. Or January.

"Yes, you. I know you fully support the CSA and everything we stand for."

That was easy. "Of course."

"Well, then, you'll be happy to be our spokesperson."

An inkling of unease tickled Marisa's gut. "What do you have in mind?"

The old guy hitched his pants and met her gaze squarely. "We voted unanimously to sponsor you in the Miss Snowflake Pageant as our representative."

They *what*?

He held up his hand. "Hear me out. We have money in the advertising budget and couldn't agree on how to spend it. Ads in The Independent Record don't bring in a lot of new customers. We need something to kick it up a notch."

"No."

"Mike said you'd say that."

"Then he should have voted against."

Bob pushed through as though she hadn't spoken. "So we discussed it, looking for something that would make you change your mind."

She crossed her arms and widened her stance. "Uh huh."

If she did it, she'd see a lot of Jase. Find out if there was any residual spark from their whirlwind romance in Kenya. Did she want to see Jase? Yes.

No.

Bob spread his arms wide. "Look at me. I'm no super-model. I can't compete."

She took in his squat five-foot-five stature, baggy cargo shorts, and plaid flannel shirt, and tried to bite back a grin. "Pretty sure you don't have the requisite girl parts." To say nothing of a little fashion sense.

"So you'll do it?" He tilted his head to the side and waggled his bushy eyebrows.

Probably thought it was a come-hither look. "No. I think you should make a run for it. Squash the gender inequality of such a pageant. You've got great ideas for agri-tourism stops in Lewis and Clark County. You'd do the CSA proud."

"Nice speech." Bob shoved his hands back in his pockets. "But gender equality is a fight for another day. This pageant is a girly thing."

"And many women are part of the CSA." Most of them were married, though, and forty-plus. Not what the Miss Snowflake pageant was looking for. It hadn't taken half an hour on their website to figure it out. Yeah, she'd looked.

"Do be serious, Marisa. Think of the good you could do."

That's what she thought in Kenya. Or what she thought she'd been thinking until Jase challenged her. Mucking in the soil, teaching orphans how to grow food from seed, how to mix animal dung with the dirt to create a better growing environment. How could he have seen that as wrong? As self-serving?

Her conscience stung. He hadn't been against her project. He'd challenged the reasons she'd wanted it captured on film. To exploit the kids stuck in poverty to advance her career. To make her look good, he'd said. Like the saving angel.

But the kids needed saving. They needed help. The filth and disease and despair still clawed at her dreams, cascading her into nightmares. How could her intervention be wrong?

"Marisa? Is it something I said?"

She blinked and brought Bob's face into focus. "Sorry."

"The board talked about what you're doing for the families on assistance."

"Doing *with* them. Not for them. They're doing it themselves."

"Semantics."

"No, an important difference. I just allowed them access to what used to be a lawn I had to mow. They're using it to grow food, and it saves me time."

Bob tipped his head back and a laugh bellowed out. "Oh, don't give me that. Don't forget I drive out past your place every day. I've seen you in the garden. There's no way you spend less time than you did mowing once a week. I bet your John Deere used to do that space in half an hour, if that."

There wasn't enough lawn left to speak of. She'd sold the mower and bought a non-motorized contraption for the remaining postage stamp-sized bits. But he didn't need to know.

"Doesn't matter." Marisa shrugged. "I hate mowing."

"The point is you care about food. Lots of our CSA growers are just trying to make enough money to stay on the land. Farming isn't their passion the way it is yours. You inspire them."

"That's... nice." Dumb answer, but he'd caught her off guard. She hadn't kept the assistance plots a secret. Not that she would have been able to, when the land she'd turned over stretched from the highway to the house along both sides of the driveway. Difficult to hide the gardens themselves, let alone the half dozen women and piles of kids that descended upon them more evenings than not.

Bob leaned closer. "We want you to represent us in the pageant. This is an important opportunity to grow the CSA, not only in subscriptions but our team as well. People need to know about the benefits we offer. They need to know healthy fresh food doesn't have to cost the earth."

Oh man. She really-really-really didn't want to do this. Not with Jase snapping pictures every time she turned around, silently berating her every choice. Or not so silently.

But what did she care about Jase's opinion? He'd lost any right to tell her what to do. To be fair, he'd never had it. She'd let his attitude run her life long enough.

"The board has a carrot to offer you."

Marisa narrowed her eyes at Bob.

He grinned. "A Scarlet Nantes."

"Ha." Thought he was cute, poking fun at the variety of carrot she'd chosen to grow for the CSA this year. Hadn't the clients kept asking for them, though?

"We'll support the school lunch program in your name."

A second ago she'd been wavering. "No."

A puzzled frown crossed Bob's face. "But you care about these kids. Don't you?"

That would be handing a boatload of ammunition to Jase. "I don't want my name attached to it. It's not about me." Never had been.

"But—"

Marisa pressed her fingers to her temples. Jase needed to get out of her head. Was it wrong to do good? Or only if she benefitted as well? But how could she do good if she avoided opportunities like this? What did God want of her?

But to act justly and to love mercy and to walk humbly with your God.

Could she retain humility while competing in a beauty pageant?

"Bob, I'll need to think about it. Pray about it."

His eyes brightened, and he opened his mouth.

Marisa held up her hand. "I'll get back to you in a day or two. I want to make sure if I do it — and it's a big if — that I'm doing it for the right reasons."

"You'll do what's right. You have a passion for food. For the kids."

Water circled the drain, each revolution taking her closer to going down with it. She could still extricate herself. But did she want to?

CHAPTER 4

The parlor of the historic main building of the Grizzly Gulch Resort lay strangely quiet, considering nearly two dozen women inhabited the space. A few chatted quietly in corners. Jase had never expected to be able to hear the classical music his dad insisted piping into the room.

He gripped his camera. Registration for the Miss Snowflake Pageant closed in half an hour. Had he really expected Marisa to come? She'd given up modeling. His brain skittered away from the fact that he'd been responsible for that. So why would she do this?

To see him again. To see if they still had chemistry.

He didn't need her here every day to know it still existed. That moment in front of The Parrot two weeks ago told him it was mutual. Even without the pageant, he could find her again, could try to make amends. Why had he waited?

The front door swished open and Avalon floated in, wearing a short skirt and fluffy sweater. How could he have forgotten her? Why hadn't he wondered why *she* wasn't here yet? Marisa had stolen his brain.

Avalon allowed herself a small smile at the sight of him. "Jase darling." She drifted closer and kissed the air on both sides of his cheeks.

"Hi, Avalon. The registration desk is just through those double doors." Which were wide open, so probably everyone had seen Avalon's entrance. He glanced over.

Kristen, seated at her desk, watched with wide eyes. She mouthed "Avalon?"

Jase gave a hopefully imperceptible nod as he backed up a couple of steps. It would never do for the contestants to believe he was favoring any one of them.

Just the photographer, Jase. It wasn't like he had any say over the outcome. His job was to record the events. Not that different from a modeling shoot, really.

"I thought you'd be happy to see me," Avalon murmured.

"I am." He blinked back to the present. "But I'm working. Your destiny awaits in the parlor." He summoned a smile as he indicated the doors once again.

She gripped his free hand — the one not holding the camera — and leaned in. She said something more, but his gaze riveted on the front door as it opened once again.

Marisa. No one pulled off casual as elegantly as she did. Dark skinny jeans ended in over-the-knee boots. Gucci, if he wasn't mistaken. A vibrant purple sweater allowed a coral top to peek out. Makeup today, just the right amount. And her hair, with loose curls tied back at the top.

Jase shifted around Avalon. Was she still talking? In just a few steps he'd reached Marisa's side. "You came." *You're gorgeous*, he wanted to say. He'd told her before. He'd said more than that.

Way too much more at JFK.

"Hi, Jase. I see I found the right place." She glanced around the entry hall, her gaze focusing on the parlor to her right. "In there, I assume?"

"Yes." He backed up a step. Gave her space. She was here to sign up for Miss Snowflake. He'd see her often for the next two months. Have the privilege of shooting her. No need to push her today.

In those boots she nearly matched his height. Unlike the surprise meeting in the walking mall downtown, today she was on her game. She gave him a breezy smile, wiggled her fingers in his direction, and strode into the parlor as though it was a catwalk. A stage. All eyes trained on her.

From what he could see of the group in the parlor, it was true. Kristen stood behind her desk with a big smile. "Marisa! Good to see you." She winked at Jase.

He was sunk. Clammy hands gripped his camera. Buzzing circled his head. God had given him another chance. He couldn't blow this one. *Please, Lord.*

"Well, that certainly puts a new spin on things." Avalon's voice dashed over him like an Arctic wave.

He'd forgotten she was here, a witness to him making a fool of himself. Had he really done that? He hadn't said anything too condemning. He hadn't raised his camera. He hadn't taken her in his arms, pulled her close, tasted her sweet lips.

That was Kenya. Before.

This was now. After.

He needed to get a grip. To wrench his gaze from

Marisa with her back to him. Her gentle curves.

"Don't humiliate me," Avalon snarled in a whisper. She strode across the entry hall and into the parlor, her head high. Straight toward Marisa.

MARISA COULD SET personal feelings aside. She'd done it on the job before, and she would do it again. She smiled at Kristen. Jase's sister. No, her event coordinator. Professional level. She could do this.

"Hi, Kristen. I'm ready to sign in."

That was probably obvious. It felt like every eye in the parlor was focused right on her. Most of all, Jase's eyes — and that woman, whoever she was. Holding hands with Jase. So much for the jolt of attraction Marisa thought she'd seen in his eyes. Fickle man.

Whatever. She'd entered because Bob and the Tomah CSA had pushed her into it. Not because of Jase Mackie.

She reached for the clipboard as Kristen passed it across the desk, but something — someone — slammed into her elbow and the clipboard clattered onto the polished oak floor.

No accident.

"Oh, let me get that for you." The willowy blonde leaned over and rescued the clipboard. She handed it to Marisa and whispered, "It's okay. I used to be rather clumsy, too."

Was Junior High back in style? Marisa shook her head. With any luck she could keep the smirk off her face.

"I'm Avalon Penhaven. And you are...?"

"Marisa Hiller. It's nice to meet you." Marisa smiled. "Excuse me, I need to fill out my form."

"Oh, I suppose I should do that, too." Avalon turned to Kristen and stretched out her hand.

A vacant Louis XIII chair flanking a bushy potted plant beckoned Marisa from the far end of the room, near an ornate door. Best of all, no empty seats were near it. Murmuring a greeting, she smiled at the girls on either side as she settled in.

To think her great-great-great-grandmother had lived in this mansion, perhaps sat in this very chair. The plastered wall with wainscoting below looked recent, but Marisa had seen photos of the room's early days and had to give Jase's parents credit for renewing the richly detailed ambience of the original.

She turned her attention to the forms. Of course, she'd gone through the online process and paid her entrance fee already — thanks to Bob — but this was the legally binding part of the process. Time to read the fine print and sign her name.

A rustle from behind her pulled her attention, and she shifted slightly in the old chair to glance at the plant. The leaves nearest her trembled.

Marisa raised her eyebrows. No draft in the room, at least none that should selectively move a few leaves and not others. Curious. She leaned back a little, the chair creaking, and gently brushed the greenery aside.

A little pixie, no more than six, stared back at her from wide brown eyes. A red-gold ponytail increased the likelihood that the child belonged to the inn and thus to Jase's family. Marisa glanced at Kristen. Yes, a likely connection.

What little girl could resist a dress-up party with a group of pretty women? Not this one, apparently. Marisa wouldn't be the one to out her. She winked conspiratorially and released the leaves to hide the imp once more.

"Oh, did you lose something in there?" Marisa nearly jumped at Avalon's cool voice, so near.

"No, not at all." Marisa smiled brightly. "I'm very interested in plants, and this healthy *Dieffenbachia* caught my attention."

Was it her imagination, or did the plant emit a tiny giggle?

"Oh, you're the entrant that's a *farmer*. Of course you'd be interested in plants. I'm pretty sure you can't eat that one, though."

Oh, really? She'd never have guessed.

She managed to bite the words back before they came out. Where did this woman get off with all her venom, anyway? All because Jase had stepped around her to greet Marisa when she arrived?

But it hadn't been just a greeting. The spark still existed between them and, apparently, it wasn't as hidden as she'd hoped. She'd work on that.

Professional level.

Avalon settled into a ladder-backed chair a few seats down, managing her short skirt efficiently. Someone had taught her poise, if not manners. She swept her multi-toned blond hair over her shoulder and caught Marisa's eye. Her perfectly sculpted eyebrows rose for an instant, and her brown eyes flashed.

Then her copper-clad lips tilted upward as though they shared a private joke. As though it would be funny if Avalon did her best every day to have Marisa discounted as a country bumpkin.

Right. The paperwork. Marisa bent her attention back to the fine print laying out all that was expected of a Miss Snowflake contestant and winner. Everything looked quite straightforward. She'd be very busy for an entire year if she won. Not allowed to get married during her reign. Well, *that* wouldn't be a problem. She signed her name with a flourish.

"Have you seen Charlotte?"

Marisa glanced up.

An elegant woman in her fifties or sixties stood in front of Kristen's desk.

A look of concern crossed Kristen's face. "I thought she was with you."

"She was playing with Liam in her room, or so I thought. She knows better than to leave without permission."

Uh-oh. Marisa didn't dare glance at the potted plant.

Jase stepped into the room. "She can't have gone far, Mom. Maybe she's over at the playground."

Mrs. Mackie looked doubtful and glanced around the space. "I didn't see her there. I thought she might have snuck over here, though. She's been playing dress-up all morning, so excited to have a real beauty pageant on the premises."

That would account for the sparkling silver bodice that had looked a few sizes too big on the tyke. Marisa couldn't very well tell on her, could she? Yet everyone seemed so concerned.

Kristen bit her lip. Her thoughts were obvious as they

crossed her face. What should a mama do? Abandon her event and go look for her child? Or trust others to locate her?

Not that Charlotte was lost, but Kristen and her family didn't know that.

"Kristen, you handle things here." Jase put his hand on his sister's arm. "I'll go find her. Don't worry. She can't have gone far."

He'd head out there, calling the child's name, over and over. That hardly seemed fair when he, too, had a job to do. Marisa bumped the plant with her elbow, hoping to send a message. Apparently the message wasn't received.

Every eye in the room seemed focused on the family gathered around the desk.

Marisa had to do something, but what? She couldn't betray the little girl, but everyone was so worried. "Why don't we all take a half hour to scour the house and grounds? With so many helping, it shouldn't take long to find her." Like two seconds, tops.

Mrs. Mackie swung to face her. "Oh, we can't have that. You young ladies are here for the pageant, nothing to do with our little one." But her face still held hope.

Some of the other women murmured and nodded their agreement to Marisa's plan. "Yes, we can help."

"For sure."

"Good idea."

Jase met Marisa's gaze in the instant before the contestants surged to their feet, breaking the line-of-sight. The women gathered around Jase and his mother for instructions.

Avalon shot Marisa a nasty look as she stood. Whether

it was for being the genius who thought of a plan everyone welcomed or for something else, Marisa didn't know. Maybe Avalon simply didn't like anything out of her control.

Oops. She should look more eager to help. Marisa elbowed the plant as she stood. She bent and set her clipboard on the floor. "Sneak out the door to the grand hall and go to the staircase," she whispered.

The leaves fluttered slightly.

Marisa joined the group around the Mackie-O'Brien family at the desk, backs to the *Dieffenbachia*. Avalon shifted away from her. Just as well. Marisa shot a glance over her shoulder in time to see a sliver of glitter flit out the door. She turned back to hear the instructions.

Jase was thinking on his feet as he divided the girls into groups and assigned parts of the mansion to search. He seemed really worried about his little niece. He'd once told her he loved working with child models more than the adults. He'd done a great job with them, too.

The first group led the way into the hall. Just as Marisa hoped, a sharp exclamation came immediately. "She's right here!"

Everyone poured into the entry. Kristen's shriek and Jase's low, steady voice were clear amidst the chatter. Marisa hung back.

"I don't know how you did that." Avalon's brown eyes narrowed. "But I do know why."

The innocence Marisa sought to bring to her face dissolved into confusion. "Pardon me?"

Avalon leaned closer. "You leave Jase Mackie alone. He's mine."

CHAPTER 5

a Thanksgiving weekend like no other.

Jase straightened his black tie as he surveyed the crowd mingling in the Helena Civic Center Ballroom Saturday evening. Men in tuxedos lifted wine glasses to women in sparkling gowns. Waiters clad in black shifted through the melee with platters high above their heads, offering drinks and hors d'oeuvres to the dignitaries of Montana's capitol city.

He shifted slightly. They'd also come to see Marisa, the great-great-great-granddaughter of the pageant's first winner. Did it seem as surreal to Marisa as it did to him? After all, she'd grown up here and no one had made a big deal of her connection from what she'd said. Not even when she'd gone to New York to model for some of the biggest names in fashion. Probably not the same as being a beauty queen in their eyes.

Mom made her way around the room to him, a glass of bubbly in her hand. "Jase! Why aren't you in the ready room taking photos of the girls?"

"Kristen has given me a strict list of what's on the official agenda, and their pep talk wasn't on it." He rubbed his camera, practically another limb. "Don't worry, I'm set to start shooting when they arrive for the banquet. And, I'll make sure to get a good cross-section of the who's who in attendance for the Record's entertainment pages."

She rested a well-manicured hand on his arm. "Good lad. We all have to do our part."

"Excellent turnout." Jase poked his chin out at the crowd. "Moving the event to the Civic Center was a great idea."

"Yes. I'm glad your father decided to expand the guest list... and the venue."

"It's an amazing building." Of course Kristen had discovered the rental space in the early twentieth-century Moorish Revival-style building, now the city's civic center. New to Helena, he hadn't bothered to figure out that the minaret he'd seen across the city hailed from such an impressive building available for events like this.

At first look he'd thought the distinctive designs in the tile floor would be out of character for a pageant ball, but he'd been mistaken. With nearly one hundred round tables dotting the space, each gowned with a sapphire blue satin cloth and lace snowflake overlay, little of the floor remained visible. Even the mezzanine levels housed tables for media.

"I hope it pays off." Dad came up behind Mom. "It still feels like a big gamble."

"Big party, you mean. What could possibly go wrong? Every bedroom in the resort is full as well."

"Don't tempt fate. I'm still not sure—"

"Don't be silly, William. It's just a series of parties we've invited many important guests to. And look. They came! Everyone will have a wonderful time toasting Montana's and Helena's anniversaries, and talk about the beauty of the Helena area. And such a delightful resort to stay at, catering to their every whim."

Dad tugged at his bow tie and glanced at Jase. "We'll see, Ruth. We'll see." He excused himself and headed for the microphone.

The chatter mellowed to murmurs.

"Welcome to the newly-revived annual tradition, the Miss Snowflake Tiara Pageant! I'm your event host, Dr. William Mackie."

Society clapped.

Jase looked at his mother and whispered, "Annual? Since when?"

"But of course! We'd be silly not to use the event to build momentum for the future. Did Kristen forget to tell you?"

His sister had neglected to tell him many things. "It doesn't matter, I guess. I'm just the photographer. It's not like I'm irreplaceable."

"Now, Jase, don't be ridiculous. You're not *just* anything. You're our son, and we want the best for you as well as for the whole family." She batted her curled eyelashes at him.

"Oh, no, you don't." He backed up a step. "I can see where this is going. Just because the first pageant's winner married the innkeeper doesn't mean history will — or should — repeat itself."

Mom laughed. "But it could. Kristen says your girlfriend is a contestant. How come you didn't tell me? Introduce me?"

She meant Avalon, of course. "It's just been a few dates, Mom. I'm honestly not that sure." He'd been even less certain since meeting Marisa again.

"But there are nineteen other women in the pageant. All beautiful. All accomplished. Surely one of them will catch your eye. If not this group, maybe next year, but I don't want to grow old and die before you give me more grandchildren."

One had caught his eye, all right. Too bad he'd blown it two years back. "So you'll keep doing this shindig until one of the women gets my attention?"

"You don't seem to be picking any on your own."

He shook his head but couldn't help the grin that poked out. "You're crazy, Mom, you know that?" He slipped his arm around her and gave her a little squeeze. "How will anyone match up to you?"

"Oh, Jason. What a nice thing to say."

It was even true. He'd met many a wealthy person who felt entitled. Not so his parents.

A rustle of silk alerted him to Kristen's arrival even before her whisper. "Shhh, you two. The contestants will be coming in the side doors in just a moment."

Time for work. "Thanks." Jase flipped his camera on and sidled along the wall.

"Please welcome Miss Avalon Penhaven, a Helena native and first runner-up in the Miss Montana pageant last year."

Polite applause as Avalon strutted in wearing a low-cut leopard-print gown, a necklace glittering against her tanned throat. She tossed her streaked blond hair over her shoulder as she paused under the spotlight and struck a pose, her eyes finding Jase's easily.

He'd like to think the saucy smile was for the camera, but he knew better.

Jase frowned. Surely Avalon wasn't whom Mother referred to when she said Jase should find a bride. He gave his head a quick shake. Focus. Nineteen more women to go.

His lens followed Avalon to her seat at the banquet's head table before swinging back to the double doors to capture the next contestant's entrance.

"Please welcome Miss Diana Riley of Great Falls, where she practices law."

The African-American beauty strode to the spotlight position and pirouetted gracefully for the crowd — and Jase's camera.

He settled in to work as contestant after contestant was introduced, trying not to listen for Marisa's name. This was a live photo shoot, and certainly not the first event he'd recorded. He knew what needed to be captured.

"And finally, please welcome Miss Marisa Hiller of Helena, a graduate of Yale and currently a local organic farmer."

To look at her here, in her element, he'd never have guessed she liked to play in the dirt.

Her coral gown swirled nearly to her knees as she pivoted. Brown hair, loosely curled, floated back to her shoulders as she tilted her head and smiled for the camera.

Straight into his eyes.

That color looked amazing on her, drawing out the sparkle of her brown eyes. He'd thought the purple from registration day had done her justice, but here she'd found her true match.

Realizing he'd taken more photos of Marisa than any other contestant, he lowered the camera.

The applause died away.

"Thank you, lovely ladies, for joining us here this evening. Let us ask God's blessing over our dinner."

By the murmurs of the gathering, not many were used to grace being said, even at Thanksgiving.

Wait staff began the task of distributing salads as the chatter picked up.

Jase had snuck a salad and roll before the event, and a plate full of turkey and trimmings would be awaiting him in the warmer. Tonight he wasn't honored family or even a guest. Tonight he was an employee.

MARISA SLIPPED BACK into the ready room to see several contestants gathered around Avalon. The chatter faded as Avalon's narrowed gaze met hers.

Competition was nothing new, but this was crazy. Top models competed for contracts all the time. Competed for the featured spotlights once they were in the catalogue. It wasn't anything personal.

Not like this. Avalon seemed happy to be everyone's friend except hers. Not that Marisa wanted that relationship, but still. She was only here because Bob and Mom had coerced her.

"You did a lovely job on your speech."

Marisa turned to see Kristen. "Thank you."

"No, really." The redhead bounced. "I'd never given food that much thought before. I mean, I know I should avoid fast-food places if I want to keep my shape, but I never really thought there was any harm in taking Charlotte and Liam sometimes so they could have a treat and run off some energy in the attached playground."

"I've learned it's important how we use the word *treat*."

Kristen's eyebrows pulled together. "Yes, I see that. I'm sure I'll learn so much from you during the pageant. I just wanted you to know I'm so happy you joined the group."

The back of Marisa's head suddenly felt itchy. Probably because Avalon's eyes were burning holes in it.

"Would you come over to the resort one day for lunch, you and your mom? I'd love to pick your brain on the topic of food."

"What a lovely invitation, but perhaps it would be best if we kept our relationship on a professional level during the competition. I wouldn't want anyone to think I was trying to sway you so I'd look more favorable."

"Oh, you're so right." Kristen lowered her voice and glanced past Marisa. "And I know who would see too much into it, too. Just because she's been dating my brother."

They were actually going out? Marisa's heart tightened in her chest. If that was the kind of girl that had caught Jase's attention lately, Marisa stood no chance with him. Not that she wanted him, but it was hard to deny the chemistry that flashed between them every time their eyes met. Hard for *her* to deny. Apparently Jase had no such problem.

With a start Marisa realized Kristen was still talking.

"Our mother has decided it's time for Jase to settle

down and get married. Look out anyone who's lucky enough to get Mom's undivided attention. The Penhavens are an old Helena family, too."

Why was Kristen telling her all this? "So your mother's in favor, then?" Not that it was any of her business.

Kristen's laugh bubbled free. "Of Avalon? Jase has been keeping it from her. I'm not sure why, but I suspect it's so Mom doesn't start planning the wedding just yet."

Marisa forced a smile. "I know what mothers can be like when they get their hooks into something. Well, you saw how mine practically forced me into the pageant. Mom and Bob Delaney."

"Bob Delaney?"

"The man from the CSA. He attended with my mother this evening, but I'm sure you had too much on your mind to notice them." Bob actually cleaned up pretty well, all things considered. Who knew the guy could pull off a suit, even if it had been new last century? "Speaking of them, Mom's waiting for me in the foyer. I should get going."

Kristen rested her hand on Marisa's arm. "I, for one, am glad she helped me talk you into competing. Half the people in this room came only to get a good look at you."

"Oh, I don't know about that. I grew up here. I doubt anyone is that fascinated."

"But you're a successful model."

Marisa shrugged. "No one in Helena cares much about that. As far as most people know or care, I went back east to go to college, get a job, and do a bit of traveling. Now I'm home."

Kristen's eyes widened. "But you're Calista and Albert's great-great-great-granddaughter."

"Trust me when I say, no one is interested. It's just a fun old family story only a few historians in town care about."

"Until recently."

Until Kristen's advertising campaign had plastered the information across the media. "They'll forget again as quickly."

"You underestimate yourself."

"Me?" Marisa pulled back. "I don't think so. I'm a realist, is all. I grew up here. You didn't. I don't get my confidence from what people think of me, but of what God thinks. To Him I am always His cherished princess, regardless of whether I win or lose in the eyes of society." A hardwon foundation.

Kristen's eyes misted. "What a beautiful way to look at it."

"It's worth far more than a tiara." And it would pay for Marisa to remember her own words. She slipped her arms into her coat sleeves.

"Marisa? Almost ready?" Mom stuck her head into the ready room.

"Getting a ride home with Mama?" Avalon asked, gliding past.

Mom shifted out of her way.

"I sure am." With no need to explain it away, either.

Avalon fluttered fingers and eyelashes at Marisa as she swept out. "Jase, darling, there you are. I'm ready to go now."

"I don't know what he sees in her." Kristen walked away, shaking her head.

Yeah, Marisa could do without following the happy couple out to the civic center's parking lot, but Mom was back in sight, beckoning. With a sigh, Marisa trailed her mother into the foyer, where Jase was helping Avalon into a fur coat. Fake or not? No doubt Avalon could make a case for either.

Bob swaggered over and grasped Marisa's hands. "Good job, kiddo. You made us proud."

Avalon laughed.

Pretty sure it was aimed at Bob, but Marisa wasn't about to check. She didn't want to see Jase's reaction to know whether he agreed with Avalon or not. She leaned down and placed a kiss on his cheek. "Thanks, Bob. Ready to head out?"

"Yep. Snow's been coming down steady while we were inside. Real pretty out now. I'll bring the car around."

Snow. Just the thought raised Marisa's spirits. "No need. We can all walk out."

"Not in them shoes, you can't. Unless you have boots along?"

Marisa glanced at her strappy heels and sighed. "Good call. Mom and I will wait right here." Beside Avalon, apparently.

Jase's Jetta was the first to glide to a stop. He hopped out and came around to open the car door for Avalon. Smirking, Avalon wiggled her fingers at Marisa as she slid into the leather interior.

Marisa waved back, trying to look more genuine than she felt.

CHAPTER 6

*I*don't see why your parents want real trees. They need watering and the needles fall off." Avalon stared at the crowded tree lot set up in the parking area of Summit Collision. A crew had brought hundreds of conifers down from the Flathead Valley for sale.

Jase let Charlotte and Liam out of the crew cab's back seat. "Stay close now, you two."

"We will, Sir Uncle Jase." Charlotte's brown eyes glinted up at him, her hair peeking out from under a white stocking cap.

"Grandpa wants tall trees." Liam looked around, eyes wide, then tucked his mittened hand into one of Jase's while Charlotte claimed the other.

Avalon narrowed her gaze at the kids then slid both of hers, clad in suede gloves, into the pockets of her coat.

Well, he hadn't exactly invited her. She'd called him and asked what he was doing, and he'd told her. He couldn't very well tell his niece and nephew they were no longer welcome to come along, could he?

"There's a tree." Liam pointed.

Charlotte skipped in place. "Lots of trees, silly. We have to see every single one of them before picking."

"But I want hot chocolate. You promised, Unca Jase."

Jase swung the little boy's hand. "I did promise, but Charlotte is right. First we have to find the trees your grandparents asked for."

"What are we looking for, then?" asked Avalon. "It can't take too long to see the selection."

"A twelve-foot blue spruce for the reception room bay, a Scotch pine for the banquet hall, and another for the penthouse." Jase started down the first row.

When Charlotte pulled free and skipped ahead, Avalon slipped her hand into the crook of Jase's arm. He grinned down at her, and she gave him a tentative smile in return.

The crisp winter air glistened around them as they strolled the lot. He could do this. He didn't have to keep thinking about Marisa. Avalon would warm up to the kids, and they'd have a great afternoon together.

Jase squeezed Avalon's hand. "What about you? Want a tree for your condo?"

She swept his words aside. "No, I have an artificial, of course. White pre-lit with blue and silver glass balls. You?"

He inhaled deeply, savoring the scent of fresh-cut trees. He'd never taken the time to know one conifer from another. But now? It was time to turn over a new leaf. "I donated my artificial to a charity fundraiser before I left New York, along with a bunch of other stuff. It's time for me to move up." He stepped closer to the nearest tree and fingered a cluster of long needles, upswept from a sturdy trunk. "Maybe something like this."

"A pine?"

He read the tag, confirming Avalon's words. "Yes. Doesn't it smell awesome? Like hiking in the mountains."

"I like this tree you picked, Unca Jase." Liam's earnest brown eyes looked up at him.

"Me, too, buddy. Shall we get it for my apartment?"

His nephew nodded. "Can I help you descrate it?"

"Decorate, little boy." Avalon shook her head.

Jase nudged her. "Aw, it's cute."

"No, it's not. Don't encourage him. He needs to learn to speak correctly."

Liam tugged at his sleeve. "Can I, Unca Jase?"

"Sure, buddy. We'll get your mama to give us a hand." Genius idea, that. Kristen would make the tree gorgeous, and he'd simply have to supply snacks and pop.

Belatedly, he remembered Avalon. He turned his best smile on her. "You, too, of course."

"No, thanks. I find the smell somewhat overwhelming, frankly. I don't think I could stand to be working around it for long."

"Allergies?" He tilted his head. "I'm sorry."

She pulled back. "Me? No. I just don't like that outdoors smell."

Why had Avalon agreed to join him and the kids for this expedition, then? It seemed he couldn't do anything right by her. Why did he even try?

Jase gazed into Avalon's beautiful brown eyes. Why did *she* try?

Her gaze grew wary. "What are you thinking, Jase darling?"

He shook his head. This wasn't the time to get into

it, to discuss their feelings for each other — or the lack of them. Why pretend to be a couple when obviously the spark was lacking? Avalon was so selfish she didn't seem to notice her rude tone. Or did she do it on purpose?

Jase broke eye contact. "Let's pick out the trees my parents want and get them loaded into the truck."

She nodded, wrapping her arms around her middle and shivering.

If that was a hint she wanted him to put his arm around her, she had another think coming. Not with four trees to get and two kids to keep an eye on.

"Come on, buddy." Jase turned to Liam. "Let's take the tag from this one while we look for a taller one for Grandpa."

Liam. *Charlotte.*

Where was she? A cold chill clawed through Jase as he pivoted, scanning the area. Trees stood in clumps all around him, like a small forest, obscuring his view. He swallowed panic. "Did you see where Charlotte went?" he asked, as casually as he could muster.

"Charlotte?" Avalon echoed, turning to look around her. "She was here a minute ago."

Thankfully, she took him seriously.

Liam looked up with anxious eyes.

Jase knelt beside the boy. "Do you see her, buddy?"

The little guy shook his head.

"Well, she can't be far. We'll find her." Surely she'd skipped around the end of the row and would reappear any second, unaware she'd caused him any alarm.

Why hadn't he paid better attention to the children?

This wasn't the time or the place to get distracted with thoughts of his love life... or lack of it.

"That child just likes to make the adults worry," Avalon stated. "Didn't she run off on registration day, too?"

Charlotte hadn't said where she'd been hiding that day, just that she wanted to see the pretty ladies.

"There at least she was at home. Here, not so much. Let's get to the end of the row, then you head right and I'll go left and we can each look down the rows until we spot her. She can't have gone far."

Avalon sighed. "Of course."

Jase tugged Liam with him as he hurried up the row. Charlotte had to be nearby. Didn't she?

"THIS DOESN'T LOOK like a Christmas tree." Davy shoved both hands deep into jacket pockets.

Marisa tipped her head. "You don't think so?"

"No." The eight-year-old shook his head. "There's no lights or ornaments."

His mom laughed. "When we get it home, we'll get it trimmed, Davy-boy. You'll see."

Lila tucked her mittened hand into Marisa's. "Will it be be-yoo-ti-ful?"

Marisa knelt. "It will be even prettier than that. Did you have a real tree last year?" She glanced up at Bren.

The young single mom puffed out her breath. "Nope. No tree at all." She grimaced. "We had nothing."

"This year is going to be different. Some of the ladies from church put together a box of ornaments for you. Now all we need is a tree to hold them all." Marisa reached for the tree she'd shown Davy. "I think this one will be fine. I've always loved a grand fir."

Lila tugged at Marisa's other hand. "Look! There's a Christmas angel."

Marisa peered around the clump of trees to see a familiar pixie wearing white leggings and jacket. Those red-gold curls peeking out from a white cap could only belong to the Mackie family. "Charlotte?"

"Hi." Charlotte's brown eyes assessed Marisa then looked at Lila and back. "You're pretty like a princess."

Bren chuckled.

"Thank you, Charlotte." Marisa straightened. "Is your mommy here somewhere? She must be wondering where you are."

Charlotte waved a hand. "Sir Uncle Jase is over there."

Marisa's heart skipped a beat.

Lila reached out and touched Charlotte's hair. "You look like an angel."

"I'm not. See?" She twirled around. "I don't have any wings."

Lila turned around too. "Me either. No wings." Both little girls spun in circles. Lila collapsed in a heap, giggling, and Charlotte stumbled against her.

They might not be cherubs, but the glee of little girls was hard to surpass. Marisa couldn't help the grin that spread across her face as the two became fast friends.

"Girls." Davy shook his head, frowning. "They're not half as funny as they think they are."

At that, the two clung to each other in a fit of giggles. "We're funny!" hiccuped Lila.

Jase must be here somewhere. This child had the most adventuresome spirit and obviously trusted everyone. Marisa glanced up and down the row they stood in. Several groups examined trees, but Jase was not among them.

Marisa held out her hands to the little girls. "Come on, Charlotte. Let's go find your uncle. He must be worried about you."

"Okay."

Marisa glanced at Bren. "I'll be right back. This will only take a minute."

"I'll guard the tree." Davy struck a kung fu pose as another family neared.

Marisa grinned as she strode to the end of the row with the pixies skipping along on either side. She turned left and all but ran into someone. Someone she knew, and it wasn't Jase.

"There you are, child." Avalon's eyes glittered as she stared down at Charlotte. "Your uncle is looking for you."

Jase was here with Avalon? Marisa's gut plummeted. She glanced around, unsure of whether or not she actually wanted to see him after all.

"Come along then." Avalon didn't reach for Charlotte, just beckoned with a toss of her head.

Charlotte looked down and tightened her grip on Marisa's hand.

Oh great. She was going to get in the middle of this whether she wanted to or not. She summoned a smile for Avalon. "Which way?"

"I can handle it from here."

The smile stayed in place by a force of will. "I'm sure you can but, as you see, she wants me to come along."

Marisa, still holding an imp by each hand, followed as Avalon shrugged and walked away, her high-heeled boots clicking against the pavement.

A few rows of trees later, Avalon stopped. "I found her," she announced.

Jase appeared with Liam at hand. He knelt. "Charlotte! You had me so worried." He seemed to notice Marisa for the first time. "Thank you."

His smile took her breath away.

He focused on Lila. "Who have we here?"

"This is my friend." Charlotte released Marisa to pull Lila forward. "Can she come have hot chocolate with us?"

Avalon made some unintelligible sound.

Jase grinned at Marisa. "I don't know. Can she?"

"Maybe not today, girls." No way was Marisa going to wedge into a date with Jase and Avalon, even if the children were instant friends. "We left Lila's mom and brother guarding our tree. We'd better get back to them."

Charlotte tipped her head and peered at Lila. "Where's your daddy? It's a man's job to get a tree. My grandma said so. That's why she sent Sir Uncle Jase."

Lila's lower lip came out and she shrugged. "I don't got a daddy."

"Everybody has a daddy."

Time to intervene. "Lila doesn't. Not anymore." Where the men who'd fathered Bren's children had ended up, no one knew. But at least Bren had hope for the future now. Marisa had made arrangements even Bren didn't know about yet. "For that matter, I don't have a daddy either. He died and went to heaven a long time ago."

"We'll have to make sure you and your new friend get a

58

chance to play soon, Charlotte. Okay? As for the tree, I'm sure her mommy and Marisa can manage it just fine." He looked at Marisa with eyebrows raised. "Right? Or do you need a hand?"

"We're good." Jase didn't mean it anyway. Not with Avalon there, one hand resting on his shoulder while he crouched beside Charlotte. "Thanks, anyway." She turned away, tugging Lila with her.

"You can't mean it, Jase," she heard Avalon say. "Look at that child's clothes. She'd be a bad influence on your niece. That family obviously doesn't have a speck of money. If you can even call it a family without a father."

Anger flared as Marisa pivoted. "A family is what you make it. It doesn't disappear just because a parent dies or walks out. Bren does the best she can with her kids, even without a lot of income. Don't judge someone unless you've walked a mile in their shoes." She fixed a glare at Avalon then shot more venom at Jase, just for being with her. Even though he'd been nice to Lila.

"Come on, sweetie. Let's go get that tree."

Avalon's laugh sounded forced. "Well, then." She took Jase's arm. "Someone has issues."

Someone sure did, and it wasn't Marisa. "Did you need to be so rude?"

Avalon's eyes widened and her full lips pulled into a pout. "Why, Jase—"

"That little kid can't help it she was born into a poor family, any more than you can help being born into a rich one." Not that the Penhavens had the resources his family had. Hmm. Was that why Avalon tried so hard to keep him in sight?

Enough, though. He wasn't in love with her. Never had been. Why had he allowed himself to keep returning to her presence? "Avalon, we need to stop seeing each other."

Twin red spots rode high on her cheeks, and it wasn't just the chilly air. "It's all *her* fault, isn't it?"

"Marisa? No." But wasn't it, partly? It had taken seeing her again to remind him of what real love could look like. "I've known for a while that you and I didn't have a future together. It was... comfortable to keep seeing you."

"Comfortable?" She all but spat the word at him.

Wrong word? But he'd said it now. This wasn't going how he'd expected. "I'm sorry."

"Not as sorry as you're going to be." She pierced him with a glare then stalked away from him and the children with her clacking high heels.

"Avalon, wait! I'll pay for the trees and take you home."

"Don't put yourself out. I'll get a cab."

"Sir Uncle Jase?" Charlotte tugged on his hand.

He pulled his gaze from Avalon's retreating back and glanced down at his niece. "What, sweetie?"

"That's not a very nice lady."

CHAPTER 7

$\mathcal{I}$t looks lovely, dear." Marisa's mom looked around the living room. "I always wished we had a fireplace in this farmhouse, but never more than when it's Christmas."

Marisa smiled in satisfaction. "Santa always managed to find my stocking, even though it just hung from a hook under the shelf." She winked at Mom. "And a fireplace without a home, without a family, isn't worth much. We had one in the apartment in New York. It took up space we could have used for an extra chair. Glory kept a bunch of candles in it until Jean needed a place for another bookcase."

"Right in the fireplace?"

"Yep." Did she miss New York? Frequent trips to Milan and Paris, to say nothing of exotic locations for shoots? Kind of. Mostly she missed what might have been.

Enough of that. Jase had gone Christmas tree shopping with Avalon. Obviously no future there.

"If you want to get out Gran's Christmas runner for the

coffee table, I'll make us some hot cocoa." Mom headed toward the kitchen. "We can put on an old holiday movie and enjoy the rest of the evening together."

"Sounds good. Is it in the trunk in your room?"

"Yes," called Mom. A clink from the kitchen announced a pot landing on the stove. No hot chocolate mix in boiling water for Mom. Nope, she'd be heating milk and whisking in Dutch cocoa and sugar plus a pinch of salt.

Marisa trotted up the stairs in her bunny slippers and opened the door to her mother's bedroom. The trunk was already open, having given up several boxes of vintage glass balls. The red-and-green Log Cabin quilted runner lay under the wooden box containing Calista's memorabilia.

Her hand slid over the smooth wood. Would she truly follow in her triple-great grandmother's footsteps? What advice would Calista have for Marisa? She'd say that winning wasn't everything. She'd encourage Marisa to follow her heart and give love a chance, just as she had done over a hundred years before. It had been a different world back then. Calista had made the best decisions she could for the era.

The latch popped open and Marisa removed the box's contents. She picked up the newspaper clipping declaring Calista the Snowflake Queen and telling how she gave it up because of her love for Albert and the little orphan child. She'd relinquished the tiara to make a home.

Marisa pulled out the sheet music for *Away in a Manger*, yellow with age. She'd already decided to play the song on her flute. Why not have this original document on her music stand, even though she didn't need it? She knew the carol by heart, every nuance, every embellishment. It had been a family favorite ever since it'd been written, just a few years before the first Miss Snowflake Pageant.

Marisa tucked the other pieces back in the box and replaced it, slipping the runner out as she did so. She tossed the fabric over her shoulder and strode to her own bedroom for her flute before jogging back down the stairs.

With the Log Cabin runner covering the coffee table, she set her case down and assembled her instrument. Wow, she hadn't played in a while. She closed her eyes and let the old carol take her away.

"Hauntingly beautiful." Mom set a tray with two steaming mugs and a plate of cookies on a side table, blinking back tears. "This is perfect."

She meant the whole atmosphere, no doubt. Baxter sprawled on his mat in the corner. The scent of pine boughs emanating from the shelf where two knitted stockings hung. The ancient artificial tree with multi-colored lights and an odd mix of glass balls and crafts from Marisa's childhood days. The blinking light garland surrounding the bay window... and headlights turning in the driveway?

Snow slanted in the glare of the lights as a vehicle crept closer to the house then stopped, lights winking out.

"Who is that?" Mom walked over to the window and peered out.

"No idea." Marisa set the flute down and headed for the front door as a sharp rap sounded. She pulled it open. "Jase?" His name caught in her throat.

He stood before her, lapels on his jacket turned up, snow frosting his bright hair. "Marisa?"

She caught herself before stepping forward into his arms, because that wasn't why he was here. Just this afternoon he and Avalon had been choosing a Christmas tree together. If that didn't tell Marisa they were a couple, nothing would.

"What are you doing here?" Without Avalon, she wanted to ask, though if he'd brought her, Marisa would have slammed the door in his face by now.

"Can I come in? Just for a few minutes?" Without waiting for an answer he moved in her direction, to the warmth of the interior.

"Um, sure. I guess." She backed up a few steps. "You can hang your coat on one of those hooks."

Mom appeared at the entrance to the living room. "Who... oh. I don't believe we've officially met."

Great. Cozy family evening with Mom speculating, and Jase... whatever he was up to. "Mom, this is Jase Mackie, the pageant photographer. Jase, my mom, Wendy."

"Do come in, Jase. Marisa will show you into the living room. I'll just fix another cup of cocoa and join you in a minute."

So much for a quick turnaround.

"Nice to meet you, Wendy. Thanks for inviting me in." He slipped the coat off his shoulders and glanced at Marisa. "Cocoa sounds great."

Marisa led the way into the other room. "Have a seat." She perched on the arm of the sofa while Jase bent to scratch Baxter's head. The dog's tail gave a few thumps. *Thanks a lot, boy.*

Jase crossed to the Christmas tree and took his time looking it over. "Didn't you pick up a cut fir this afternoon?"

"I did. For my friend."

"But... why?"

Not that he'd understand. "She'd never had a real one. I thought it was important for her kids."

Jase glanced over his shoulder. "But not for you?"

"This one has been in our family for years." Likely he could see that for himself. The style wasn't lush like new fake trees. No white twinkle lights or monochromatic theme.

"It's pretty."

Sure it was, but Mom wouldn't be out of the room much longer. "Why are you here?"

"I need to apologize to you."

That was a good start.

"I was wrong. In Kenya."

"Yes, you were." He had no idea how she'd struggled with his words. For nearly two and a half years.

"Marisa. Please. I had this idea — a wrong idea — that filming the kids in the slum was taking advantage of them. That they'd see no tangible benefit."

"But *I* would benefit." She gritted her teeth. "We've been over this."

"I was wrong. You were trying to help them the best way you knew how. I was blind."

Marisa avoided looking at him. "I don't regret it. If I had Kenya to do over again, I'd make you take the photos. Or found another photographer to bring along." Her gaze narrowed. "Probably a better idea."

"I'm trying to apologize here."

"It's too late, Jase." Marisa raised her chin and looked him in the eye. "You're only making an excuse for why a guy like you is found shooting a pageant that's sole purpose is to showcase pretty women and the causes they care about."

He stared and took a few steps closer. "You think that? You think I'm apologizing to save face for my part in this?"

"Aren't you?"

He crouched in front of the coffee table. Good thing it was between them. "No. I care about you, Marisa. I'd give anything to have a chance with you again."

She stared hard into his eyes for a long moment. "Anything?"

He hesitated.

She'd caught him in a lie. Marisa shook her head. "Nice try, Jase. Just this afternoon you were arm-in-arm with Avalon. She entered the pageant, too. Did you tell her the same thing? That you believe in what she's doing and care about her? Make up your mind. I'm not stupid."

"I'm not seeing her any more. Dating her even once was a mistake."

"You make a lot of them with women, don't you?"

He reared back. She'd hurt him, but he deserved it.

"In the past. I'm wiser now."

She laughed. "Wiser than you were this afternoon?"

"Is this a bad time to come in?" Mom's voice came from the kitchen doorway.

Marisa tore her gaze from Jase's smoldering eyes. "No, please, you have perfect timing." She couldn't let Jase hurt her again. She couldn't fall for his smooth lies.

Mom glanced from one to the other. "Why don't you have a seat, young man?" She pointed at a vacant armchair and set a candy-cane-striped mug and cloth napkin on the nearby side table. "Do you like homemade shortbread?"

Jase took another long look at Marisa before taking the proffered seat. "Thank you." He helped himself to two cookies.

Mom settled into her favorite chair, cloaked in Gran's afghan. "Now tell me about yourself, Jase. How long have you been living in Helena?"

JASE TOOK a deep breath and a sip of the hot chocolate through the mounds of whipped cream. It probably left him with a milk mustache, but nothing the napkin wouldn't cure.

"I moved here in July. My parents bought the Grizzly Gulch Resort about a year before that."

"You're Kristen's brother?"

Did he mistake Marisa's eye roll?

"Yes, I am."

"Such a lovely young lady."

This wasn't going too badly. Until he looked at Marisa and saw her staring at a spot on the floor, her jaw clenched.

"Kristen's a great sister." Maybe he could tell Wendy everything he wanted to tell Marisa. "She's married to a nice guy, and they live in Salt Lake City. Two little kids."

"You like children, then?"

He laughed. Even to him it sounded strained. "Sure do. Charlotte is six, and Liam is four. They tell interesting stories and love tickles."

"A delightful age, for sure. My daughter likes children, too."

"Mom. Enough." Marisa surged to her feet.

Wendy turned a bland face at her daughter. "Enough of what? I'm just engaging in pleasant conversation with our guest." She took a sip from her mug and turned back to Jase. "So tell me how you met Marisa."

He ignored the strangled sound as Marisa collapsed back onto the sofa. "I freelanced as a photographer for several modeling firms in New York. I shot Marisa many times, but we didn't get to know each other until a trip to Kenya about three years ago."

"Two and a half years," Marisa cut in. "Not that anyone is counting."

His heart soared. "My apologies. You're right. It was springtime. We worked on the beach for days. Swimsuits, loungewear, sundresses, hats." He paused while a dozen Marisas paraded through his memory, all of them radiant. "Spent our evenings in the hotel lounge." He looked Marisa in the eye. "Talking. Getting to know each other."

She had the most striking brown eyes with golden high-lights, perfect with her glistening brown hair. It was her natural color, or close to it. He'd never seen roots or a different shade that he could recall.

With a start he remembered her mother was in the room. He took a bite of the cookie. It all but melted in his mouth.

"And then?"

Marisa pulled to her feet. "Mom, do we have to go there?" She strode to the window.

Wendy took a sip. "I think we do."

Marisa whirled back to face them. "What happened is that I'd made an arrangement with Greg and Tammy from the mission to deliver some vegetable seeds for the orphans our last night there. You know they're always struggling for funds. Funds for them to live on, funds for them to run the ministry with." She stared hard at Jase. "I had this idea—"

"She asked me to join her, Wendy. To take photos of her with the orphans. Of her showing them how to plant and tend the seeds." He took a deep breath, still focused on Marisa's face. "This was after work, you understand. Not part of our contract."

"I just wanted to help. I thought if people could see the needs, they'd give more generously." She wrenched her gaze from his and looked at her mother. "Jase is a talented photographer," she ground out. "He could have done a fine job. He could have helped me make a real difference for those kids. Instead—"

"Instead I accused her of wanting to look good." Jase parked both elbows on his knees and ran his hands over his bent head. "I thought she was as selfish as other models I'd worked with, trying to further her own career by seeming to have a philanthropic streak."

She stalked closer to him, but he didn't look up. He heard the muffled sound on the braided rug until her pink bunny slippers stopped in front of his own gray socks.

"I went that night anyway, you know." Her tone had turned conversational, but the ice behind it hadn't completely melted. "Those kids were so excited for the seeds. We planted them together. Later Tammy sent me snapshots of the kids watering them as they grew, and enjoying the harvest."

Dear Lord, now was a good time for him to man up. Right now, while she was so close to him. Mere inches away. He stood and looked deep into her eyes, his hands somehow finding hers. "Marisa, I'm sorry. I'm the one who was selfish. I was wrong. Can you please forgive me?"

From the corner of his eye he saw Wendy slip out the doorway.

"I'll consider it." Marisa squeezed his hands but stepped back.

For the moment, it was enough, though he hadn't told her everything.

CHAPTER 8

*B*ut what if you win?" Bren Haddock planted both elbows on the kitchen table. "From what I hear, you're going to be way too busy to do everything on the farm for an entire year."

Marisa slid a plate of Mom's gingerbread men on the table.

Davy and Lila hesitated until their mother nodded then each selected a cookie from the plate.

"Here, let me put on a DVD. How about Veggie Tales, or do you want Charlie Brown Christmas instead?"

"Veggie Tales Christmas!" Davy shouted then bit the head off his cookie.

Marisa laughed. "Come on then." She led the way into the living room and turned on the program. "Do you want the Christmas tree lights on?"

"Yes!" Davy bounced on the sofa.

Marisa flipped the switch, and Lila's eyes widened. "It's pretty. So many colors."

Marisa hugged the child to her side. Would she ever have little ones of her own? Time was slipping by, even though she and Jase had started to talk again. She couldn't count on him.

Bren already nursed a mug of black coffee when Marisa returned to the kitchen and poured her own.

"Nice way to put off my question." Bren grinned. "I'm concerned about the farm and your mom, you know. Because I finally got one of those pageant books and read the whole thing. Those other girls don't have the chops to beat you."

Marisa sat and pulled her coffee toward her. "Mom and I talked about the farm before I agreed to do it. Plus it's Bob who pushed me into it."

"I know. But maybe they didn't think you'd win."

Interesting thought. *Nah*. Marisa laughed. "My mother is bedazzled. She's certain I'll take the tiara. Our ancestor won and gave it up to build a family. My mom respects that, for sure, but I can see the gleam of glory in her eyes all the same."

"But who will run the farm? I know she used to, but she leased most of it out until you came back. Now the CSA is counting on you guys."

"Bob said he'd send someone over to help when Mom needed it. He's invested, being as I'm representing the CSA and the local food movement in general."

"Yeah, but who is he going to send? Some high-schooler who doesn't know anything and doesn't show up half the time?"

Good question, actually. Marisa eyed her friend. "Any suggestions?"

Bren stabbed her thumb at her own chest and raised her eyebrows.

Marisa's cup, halfway to her mouth, paused then resettled on the table. Could Bren really pull it off? Under Mom's guidance, she probably could. Davy and Lila would have to come, too. There wouldn't be money for daycare on top of wages from the CSA.

"I don't know if we can pay you enough to make it worth your while, although I totally appreciate your offer." Marisa took a sip of coffee. "If I should win — and, in my eyes, that's a big if — they don't pay me for the time I devote. I'll still be here, working at least part time on the farm in between events all over Montana and the West talking about the many benefits of local food."

"Marisa, I'm not in it for the money. Sure, I need to pay my rent somehow, but the kids and I have been eating way better since we hooked up with you. I know several of my friends say the same. You've taught us how to grow and cook real food. Davy and Lila have hardly had any colds in the past two years. And you know how many germs go around the schools. It's not just luck they've been so healthy."

Tears dimmed Marisa's eyes. This. This was what she was born to do. What she'd wanted to do in Kenya. Simply to make a difference. Was it too much to ask?

Bren's voice softened. "I thank God every day for you and your mom. And I want to give back. I can't bear the thought that, if you're busy, things will suffer here."

"Bren, I don't know what to say." It wasn't that Marisa hadn't thought about it, but with the pageant culminating the day before Christmas, and the planting season on the farm not getting into full swing for several more months, even in the greenhouse, it'd been a discussion she and Mom were leaving until later.

"I don't know as much as you do. I don't have a fancy degree in agriculture." Bren grinned. "I don't have a fancy degree in anything, but I do have my GED, and I can take a course this winter by distance ed." She twisted the mug on the wooden farmhouse table. "It's the first thing I've found that really interests me."

Happiness leapt inside Marisa. "I'm so glad." She eyed Bren speculatively. "You thinking of doing something like this as a career choice?" Because that made all the difference. Opened up tons of possibilities.

"Maybe." Bren met her gaze. "Is that dumb? I know I can't afford a piece of land and don't know if I'll ever be able to. So I probably shouldn't even think about it."

Marisa reached across the table and squeezed Bren's hand. "There's nothing wrong with having dreams. Everyone needs them."

"But you're living yours. Aren't you?"

How much should she tell this woman who must be several years her junior? Some poor choices had given Bren two kids and no one to help her raise them, to say nothing of a life of poverty. No wonder Marisa's life must look golden to her.

Thank You, Jesus. I keep forgetting to be grateful for all the blessings I do have while I pursue the things I want. Forgive me.

"There's a funny thing about dreams," Marisa said carefully. "Whenever you achieve one, you see more dreams, more goals, on the horizon."

"I'm not sure what you're saying."

"Being back and helping Mom on the farm has been awesome. We've definitely kicked things to the next level by joining the CSA. And I'm her only child, so it's not like anyone else will inherit the farm when she dies. But if you haven't noticed, she's only fifty and not ready to retire or deed me the property. This is her home, and I don't want to stay living here as her kid indefinitely."

"Oh. That makes sense. You were away for a long time. It must seem weird to live with your mother again."

"Seven years. College, then my modeling career. Yeah, it's strange. I mean, we get along great, but…"

"No, I get it. But she can't run the farm without you, can she? It seems to take both of you plus some."

Marisa took a sip of her coffee. "I've cornered myself." It hadn't seemed so bad at first. After all, she'd worked on an organic farm in Vermont two summers during college. Her passion for fresh, local food had only grown since then. When she'd come home to lick her wounds after that horrid fight with Jase, joining the CSA with Mom had seemed so right. Safe.

That didn't make it the wrong choice. Did it?

Sure, she was making a difference for Bren and other struggling young moms. She helped provide fresh produce for dozens of wealthier families in Helena, too. But was this really what she wanted to do for the rest of her life, when needs were so great elsewhere?

Kenyan kids clamored in her brain, thrilled beyond anything she'd ever seen by the simple act of watching seeds grow.

"Marisa?"

Africa faded as the bright farmhouse kitchen came back into focus.

"I don't know, Bren. I'm not sure what God has for me long term."

Voices came from outside. Boots stomped on the deck. The farmhouse door opened, and Mom's laughter sounded, followed by a low voice.

Marisa's gaze met Bren's.

Her friend shrugged.

A second later Mom breezed into the kitchen, followed by Bob and Baxter.

Bob? What was he doing here?

THE PARROT CONFECTIONERY beckoned Jase with its bright colors and promises as he hurried down the Last Chance Gulch walking mall, collar turned up against the howling wind.

He ducked inside, the sweet aroma of dozens of kinds of candies mingling with the scent of buttery popcorn from the theater-style popper in the corner. He brushed snow off his coat, stamped it off his boots, and felt the warmth of the confectionary begin to absorb into his frozen skin.

Jase doused a bowl of chili with a shot of vinegar and another of Tabasco before sliding into a vintage booth with its worn wooden benches and metal-rimmed tabletop. He crumbled a package of crackers on top and had a sip of hot black coffee before spooning up a bite of chili. He couldn't resist arrowing through the thumbnails on the back of his camera.

The photo shoot of the Simpson family in historic Reeder's Alley had been fun, if freezing. In a few minutes, once he'd thawed out some, he'd sprint across the walking mall to his studio and see what he'd captured. Hopefully his shots would look as good — or better — on the computer as they did on the camera.

A shadow loomed over his table and Jase glanced up. "Mr. Penhaven! What brings you down to the Gulch today?"

"May I join you?"

Jase turned the camera off and slid it over. "Absolutely. Please do." Not for the first time, he examined Avalon's father's face without a clue what went on behind the shuttered lids.

The older man dug into a bowl of chili with gusto.

Jase took the hint... and the opportunity to eat his own lunch, though it didn't sit as well as he'd thought it would. What had Avalon told her father?

After a few minutes Mr. Penhaven pushed his empty bowl aside and leaned back in the wooden booth. "Avalon tells me you two had some words."

"I guess you could say that."

"She's a fine woman, young man. She just needs a strong hand to keep her in line. Do you have what it takes?"

Jase blinked. "Sir? It will take more than a strong hand. I think it will take love."

Mr. Penhaven waved his hand. "Love is a fine thing, but you know there are considerations just as important.

Breeding. Education. Placement in society." He winked. "Net worth."

Jase resisted the impulse to leap to his feet and scramble out. He clenched his hands together under the table and prayed for wisdom. For grace. "So I've been deemed an acceptable suitor for Avalon based on my family's money?" He supposed they were fairly well off. His dad's years working in New York as an investment banker had certainly been lucrative.

Mr. Penhaven chuckled. "That would be one way to put it."

It seemed so old-fashioned. So... cold. "I'm sorry, sir. When I marry, it will be for love."

"Love often follows."

Jase had once thought he could come to love Avalon. Closer inspection had proven him wrong. "It could, I suppose. But why not start with it and be sure?"

"Ah, Jase. You're thirty now, aren't you? And still a romantic at heart. You're not getting any younger, if you don't mind being reminded."

The man's condescending tone was far more abrasive than the words themselves. Jase shrugged, trying to appear casual when he felt anything but. "Thirty's a fact. God has blessed me with a wonderful career." But while he'd thought he could be happy living in Montana and running a portrait studio, the travel bug had begun to itch again.

Would he be content here with Marisa? Surely. But Avalon? The thought made him twitch in his seat.

"The other thing about love." Mr. Penhaven leaned over the table and lowered his voice. "People fall in and out of it all the time. It's not something you can count on. It's just hormones talking, after all. You need something more. Shared goals, for example."

This was not a discussion he wanted to have with Avalon's father. "You're right. A couple needs a common direction as well as love." He took a deep breath. Could he retain tact? "I don't see that your daughter and I have much for shared goals, quite honestly."

Mr. Penhaven waved the concerns away with a flick of his bejeweled hands. "She's a handsome woman, my Avalon. Her mother's looks have lasted well, I might add. My daughter will give you beautiful children and cement your family's entry into Helena society. She'll one day be the heir of everything I possess, and you will have a decent heritage of your own, I believe."

Was the man proposing a marriage in this backward way? Jase shook his head. He gulped half his cup of coffee, now lukewarm. "Mr. Penhaven, I appreciate the trust you have in me. Really, I do. But Avalon and I are unsuited for each other. There is no wedding in our future."

The older man frowned. "Let's not be hasty here."

Jase edged out of the booth and grabbed his camera. "I'm not. We've been seeing each other for several months, and I believe I speak for both of us when I say there's no point. I don't love her, and she doesn't love me." He raised a hand as Mr. Penhaven opened his mouth. "Whatever we had, it's over. Permanently so. I hate to disappoint you."

Okay, that was an outright lie. How could he accept a man like this for a father-in-law? He'd be trying to run their lives forever.

"I'm sorry to hear that."

Acceptance? Jase let out a deep breath he hadn't realized he was holding.

The man looked up. "One more thing, Jase."

"Yes?"

"The rent on your studio will be going up." With a smug smile, Mr. Penhaven slid him a legal-sized envelope. "Here's your official notification."

CHAPTER 9

I've never eaten here before." Marisa took in the interior of Lucca's Italian restaurant. She gave Jase a sideways grin. "I'm usually in a hurry when I'm in this part of town, and a bowl of chili at The Parrot fits my timeline."

Jase looked good, dressed to the max in a near-navy suit with rolled-up hems. So trendy. She should have expected that of him after all his years capturing the fashion industry. Like her, he could dress up or down depending on the situation.

"Me, too. My office is just down the walking mall, so I pop in at The Parrot frequently."

"May I take your orders?" asked the waiter.

Jase ordered an appetizer for each of them. When he turned his green eyes back on her, Marisa could barely stand to meet his gaze.

How could she know if she could really trust him now? If he'd really changed? Look at him. Dressed for New York or Paris or Milan. Not Helena, where even money wore blue jeans.

He reached across the table and captured her hands, his thumb swirling circles on the back of her hand. "You seem serious tonight."

She shook her head, trying to dislodge the melancholy, but it was difficult.

"I missed you so much," he continued softly. "And God brought you back into my life. I'm thankful."

Marisa stared at their joined hands on the snowy table-cloth as though they belonged to someone on screen. Someone not her. And yet, she tingled at his tantalizing touch. "I missed you, too," she managed to say. That much was certainly true.

"Then why so sad?"

She pushed a smile to her lips. "Introspective, is all. A lot has changed in the past month or two. I was just a farmer—"

"You've never been just *anything*, Marisa."

She met his gaze then looked down again. "I was a farmer focused on food and local families. Now I'll be contending for Miss Snowflake and you're here." In the flesh. Touching her, but not demanding. Why couldn't she let go and enjoy being with him? "It's surreal. I'll probably wake up in the morning, and it will all have been a dream."

"Are you worried about the farm when you win? You'll be busy next year. I didn't think of that when I urged you to enter."

"Bob says he's got it covered. And my families will kick in." How could she tell him she'd spent three summers focused on building a life here, but the pageant reminded her of all she'd left behind? She loved the farm, especially the chance to grow food and help feed her families. She loved each of them, but the world was so much bigger. So many other people needed access to good, real food. So many hungry kids.

"That's good, then. You've worked hard on everything. I'm glad it will survive fine while you step out for a year."

She lifted a shoulder and let it drop. "There's no guarantee I'll win, of course. Several of the other contestants are very accomplished and have causes much more mainstream than mine. Passions the judges will understand and embrace."

"You'll win."

Marisa peeked up through her lashes, and her heart caught at the expression on his face. Utter belief in her, and something more. Why couldn't it have worked out with him earlier, without that horrible fight? Her mind could replay it on demand. Word for word, gesture for gesture, emotion for emotion. He'd hurt her so badly.

A plate of steamed pesto mussels landed on the table between them, and she pulled her hands free to make room. Finally, a distraction. She went with an easier topic. "I still can't believe you ended up in Helena." She jabbed a mussel and popped it in her mouth.

Jase's face lit up. "I know. It seems so random, yet I'm certain God brought me here for a reason. Maybe I should say He brought my parents here. After all, I only followed them."

"How did that happen?"

He shrugged. "Dad retired from banking and wanted to come west. Kristen and Todd were living in Salt Lake and my parents wanted to be nearer them, but the city itself didn't appeal to either of them."

Marisa nodded. "I've flown through the Salt Lake City airport dozens of times. It doesn't entice me, either."

"Kristen says the Mormon Tabernacle is breathtaking."

"But the Cathedral of St Helena is right here. It's pretty amazing itself." And that's where they were headed in an hour. Christmas at the Cathedral with the Helena Symphony.

"I think it's one of the reasons Mom and Dad chose Helena. They can hop a flight and be at Kristen's within a couple of hours." He grinned. "I like seeing the kids oftener, too. Definitely a benefit of living out west."

"I can see that." She had nothing similar holding her in Helena. She'd been focused on the farm until the pageant thing came up. Until seeing Jase again. Both had reminded her of the bigger world outside Montana.

"What about you? What do you like best about Helena?"

Strange question on the heels of her thoughts. How invested was Jase? And did it matter? Yes, somehow it did.

Maybe the restlessness in her had more to do with him than the place. "Well, I grew up here, so for me it's home, with all the plusses and minuses that entails. I love the history of the city and all the glam." There, she'd admitted it. The glitz still called to her.

He leaned back in his chair, watching her. "I couldn't believe the state legislature building. That place is amazing. There's a lot of gold decorating all the arches and the corridor above the stairs. And those murals. Wow."

Marisa grinned. "This was definitely a cultural hotspot

in the Wild West. They had to have something to do with all the gold they panned out of Last Chance Gulch. Mom shared Calista's journals of that era with me. Fascinating to read the juxtaposition of culture and, not only wilderness, but lawlessness."

"My roots are in New York," he mused.

The way he focused on her shifted something inside her gut. Easier to look at the platter between them and select a mussel than meet his eyes. She'd always wanted to dine at Lucca's, but Italy — Milan — screamed romance at her. Who wanted to enter such a fine establishment alone or with girlfriends?

"I'm happy to have been transplanted here. I hadn't seen much of my family the past few years with all the travel on the job. Now I get to drop in for dinner with my parents several times a week, and Kristen and the kids are here at least twice a month for a few days. Getting to know Charlotte and Liam is the best."

She stared at him stupidly. "You don't live with your parents?"

"Me?" He pulled back and laughed. "No, of course not. With the resort, they need every room in the house for paying guests. I've got an apartment downtown, within easy walking distance of my studio."

Somehow she'd assumed otherwise. Why? Because she'd moved back into her own childhood bedroom?

"Besides, having her grandkids around reminds my mother that I'm not married. And then she reminds me, as though I hadn't noticed."

Whoa. "Your folks seem like wonderful grandparents. Charlotte adores your mother, from what I've seen."

Jase met her eyes. "They both love kids. Mom's always nagging me to—" His voice broke off and his gaze dropped to the platter between them.

He didn't need to finish. She knew what he meant to say.

Jase reached for her hands. "Marisa, I—"

Too soon. She picked up her linen napkin and wiped her hands. "Excuse me. I need to use the ladies' room." Maybe he'd think she hadn't picked up on the direction the conversation had veered. Maybe he'd think, at all.

THE CLOSING ARIA hung in the air amidst the golden chandeliers in the Cathedral of St Helena. The audience held its collective breath as the note faded.

Beside him, Marisa leaned forward slightly, her eyes fixed on the mezzo-soprano whose hands spread to the sky, as though the arched and gilded ceiling had ceased to separate humanity from the heavens.

The acoustics in this building were rumored to be so good a person could literally hear a pin drop anywhere within it. At this moment, wrapped in a holy hush, Jase believed it. Christmas in the Cathedral had affected him every bit as deeply as any night at the New York Philharmonic. Maybe more so.

He could do Helena. He'd always miss the Big Apple, but Helena was worth it ten times over for Marisa's sake. The void in his life had lessened since finding her again.

God was here. Not everything stirring in his soul had to do with Marisa. Plenty of it had to do with immersing in

God's nature and drawing closer to Him. Helena didn't block God's voice the way New York and its insanity did. Here a guy could think, could pray.

His gaze lingered on Marisa's profile.

Here a guy could hope. Could love.

She still held back from him a little, but his mind had jumped all the way to the altar. Maybe they could even be married right here in the cathedral. Once he'd convinced her he'd stay in Helena forever, just to be with her, she'd welcome him. He'd devastated her in the Kenyan aftermath. How could he make it up to her? Prove to her his apology was sincere?

Rustling began in nearby pews as folks gathered their coats. Jase slid his arm around Marisa. "Amazing," he whispered.

She leaned into him. Not much, but it was progress, and he'd take it. Her brown eyes glimmered in the cathedral's soft lighting as she looked up at him.

Jase pulled her a little closer and swept his lips across her forehead. "You're beautiful, Marisa," he murmured. "You belong here, in this place of magic. In this place of heaven on earth." He pulled her coat to her bare shoulders.

"I don't want to leave yet. Do you mind?" Her eyes begged his. "I need to absorb the majesty."

His heart surged. She felt as he did. How could things not work out between them? He leaned back in his seat. "Take your time."

Around them, others slipped quietly out into the night until only a few pockets of people remained.

"God among us," Marisa said quietly. "It's beyond comprehension."

"He loved us that much. Calls us to Him."

She turned to him. "It's crazy. We're not worth it."

"We are to Him."

"People say I'm beautiful." She put a finger to his lips to stop the words she had to know he wanted to say. "But God doesn't see me that way. When He looks at me, He doesn't see me. He sees Jesus."

He's missing a great view.

Oh, Jase knew it wasn't true. God knew exactly what He'd created in Marisa. Not only a woman with a beautiful face and body, but one with a personality and heart to match.

Like the fictional Christmas thief, Jase felt like his heart grew ten sizes bigger, just thinking about her.

"Do you think God cares who wins the Miss Snowflake title, Jase?" Her brown eyes looked boldly into his. "If He doesn't place the same importance on beauty as humans do, why should He care?"

He lifted his hand to her face and traced her jaw. "He cares, Marisa. He cares, not because of the title, but what He wants to do through you because of it. He has great plans for you."

She leaned into his touch, her eyes still meeting his.

"Great plans," he repeated. Plans he'd be part of. For better, for worse. For richer, for poorer. He leaned a little closer and caressed her lips with his own for a few seconds before pulling back.

As much as he wanted to pursue, this wasn't the time. Definitely wasn't the place. He rose, catching her hand and pulling her up with him.

They exited the tall arched doors of the cathedral into a

crisp winter night. The full moon hovered not far above the horizon, casting an ethereal glow over the parking area.

Even in darkness, there was light. Jesus had come into such a dark world and shone a holy light into it. He'd brought light into the darkness of Jase's soul... and into his heart.

CHAPTER 10

*M*om pulled the curtain back on the dining room window. "Everyone's starting to arrive."

Marisa arranged mocha peppermint pretzel cookies on the tray and tilted her head for closer examination. She and Mom had been baking for several days, preparing their annual sledding party at the farm for their families. Okay, so it was only the third year. That still counted for annual, right?

The front door opened, and Bren stuck her head in. "Need some help in here?"

"No, we're good. Bob's in charge of the camp stove to keep the cocoa hot."

"Okay, I'll keep the troops happy until you get out here." The door clicked behind Bren.

Marisa turned to her surprise helper. "Make sure it doesn't burn. You have to keep the flame low, and stir a lot."

Bob hitched his pants and grinned. "I've got it. It's not like this is the first time I've been near a stove."

She supposed. He'd been a widower for probably ten years. Odds were good he'd managed to cook something without burning it in that amount of time.

"Unless I take a few spins down that hill myself and forget." He winked.

Marisa rolled her eyes but couldn't hold back a grin. For all his idiosyncrasies, she liked the guy. Not, apparently, as much as her mother did. Who knew?

"You also can't eat all the cookies. I think Mom packed you a big enough box to take home, so here you have to share with the kids."

"Rules, rules. Aren't they made to be broken?"

"Everything ready, then?" Mom crossed the room to stand beside Bob, but she was looking at Marisa.

Marisa nodded. "I'm ready to bundle up and head outside." Had she been crazy to invite Jase? Worse yet, Kristen's crew? Would anyone see this as trying to sway the pageant? But the Mackie family wasn't judging. They had no real power over who won. Everyone had friends.

She headed for the hall closet and slipped into her purple snow pants, then her boots and parka. Not as cute as the white ski suit her sponsor had provided for the contestants' day at the Great Divide Ski Area. Next week. She blocked the thought and grabbed her mitts from the basket before opening the door.

The crisp air smelled of snowflakes and wood smoke. Soft snow sifted gently, adding a fresh layer to the several inches that fell overnight. Davy and one of his buddies already had a snowball the size of a wheelbarrow beside the driveway and were busy rolling another one, presumably for the snowman's body, while Baxter growled and danced around the growing ball.

Lila, blond hair flying out from under a red stocking cap, flopped on her back in a fresh patch of snow, swinging her arms and legs to create a snow angel. She'd no sooner struggled to her feet, marring the angel's skirt, when Davy rolled over the spot with his snowball.

"Mommy! Make him stop."

Marisa grinned. Those must be Lila's favorite words.

Another car churned down the driveway and parked beside the greenhouse. That made all of her families.

Right behind it came a white Jetta and a gray Subaru.

Jase. He'd come. Now he'd see what she really did here. What was important to her. They happened to be the same things Avalon scorned. Yes, he'd broken things off with Avalon and turned to Marisa. But still, would he really understand? This would be his test, to see if he could relax and enjoy these wild kids and their moms, who all lived on social assistance.

Even Bob was about to get a real eye-opener.

Hopefully the day would be perfect. The weather certainly was.

Jase emerged from the Jetta as the Subaru pulled in beside him. He waved at Marisa and opened the other car's back door. Charlotte and Liam tumbled out then ran to join in the fray. Charlotte and Lila grabbed each other's arms and jumped up and down, shrieking, like the long lost bosom friends they obviously were.

Marisa crossed the yard, linking Bren's arm and towing her along as she went. Icy. They should have sprinkled sand on the parking area.

Kristen emerged and rounded the vehicle to stand between Jase and a tall blond man. "Marisa! Thank you for inviting us. I'd like you to meet my husband, Todd."

"I'm so glad you came. Nice to meet you, Todd. This is my friend Bren, the mother of Lila, whom you may have heard about."

Kristen beamed and held out her hand to Bren. "I'm Kristen. Charlotte could hardly wait to come today and see her bestest friend in the whole wide world again."

The two little girls now pelted the bigger boys with handfuls of snow. This could not end well.

Jase slipped his arm around Marisa and gave her a little squeeze. "You look awesome."

She leaned on his shoulder for a second. "Thanks." She pulled away with an apologetic grin. Better get things going before the little girls found themselves the targets of expertly formed snowballs. At the moment the bigger kids were in the process of heaving the third ball up to form the snowman's head.

"Here." Bob held out a sack to Davy. "Here's some stuff to finish it off, if you want."

Davy dumped the bag into the snow and sorted through it. "Yeah!" he yelled as he jabbed a carrot into the snowball. It wobbled. "Now he just needs a hat and scarf." He pulled his stocking cap off.

"Davy, no!" Bren called. "You need it to keep warm yourself."

The boy tried to get it on the snowman's head, but it slid off, too small. With a shrug he slammed it back on his own head, then unwound the scarf from around his neck and draped it around the snowman.

Marisa laughed at the expression on Bren's face. "He'll be fine. I can get him another scarf if he gets cold."

"Kids," Bren muttered.

"Come on everyone," Marisa called. "It's time to head up the hill. Do you have your sleds and toboggans?"

A cheer went up, and Baxter woofed in excitement.

LIAM SQUEALED the whole way down the hill, nearly deafening Jase as the tube spun in circles. They slid to a stop mere feet away from the snowman. Oops. He'd need to make sure to steer it farther left next time. As though those doughnuts could be steered.

"Did you like that, buddy?"

"Yes!" shouted Liam, struggling to his feet. The poor kid was nearly as wide as he was tall in that padded snowsuit, only his bright red nose and sparkling eyes visible.

Sheltered from the hill and straying sleds, Wendy and Bob sat in lawn chairs beside a bonfire, a camp stove set up on a nearby table.

"Want to warm up, buddy?"

Liam shook his head and grabbed the towrope.

Jase waved at Marisa's mom and turned to help his nephew pull the inner tube back up the hill. Once at the top, the boy coaxed his daddy onboard and headed down again. Jase scanned the area. Where was Marisa?

She went flying past him down the hill, two little kids between her knees on a long plastic sled.

Jase grinned and commandeered a nearby saucer. She was a hard one to catch. Always busy. Always making sure everyone was having a good time. The perfect hostess.

The perfect girlfriend.

Mr. Penhaven was right in one thing. Jase was, in fact, thirty. Definitely time he found the right woman, married her, and started a family. Two months ago it had been the farthest thing from his mind, but in the past two weeks, it was all he could think about.

He'd enjoyed every minute he'd been able to spend with Marisa since the night her mother had given him the chance to speak his mind. But she'd been busy, and so had he. They hadn't had a lot of time to talk. Had she really forgiven him? Because it seemed a little like she still held him at arm's length.

He grinned as trees and clumps of snow whizzed past. Not completely at arm's length. Close enough to believe they might have a future together, but how? Where? She was a Montana girl. She'd created a life for herself here while he found himself longing to go back to New York. Maybe not the city itself, but the opportunities there.

He was a good photographer. He knew it. The modeling agencies knew it, too. The people of Helena didn't want to pay the prices he could command back East. But it wasn't all about the money. Since that day in front of the luggage carousel in JFK airport, he'd thought a lot about charity. He'd gone back to Kenya. Returned to hunt down Tammy and Greg and see what they were really doing with the street kids. He'd been sending money to Hope's Promise every month since, never daring to ask if they had Marisa's contact information. He didn't want it to seem as though he'd been doing a good deed to regain her affection. No, he'd discovered need he'd never noticed before, and God had given him compassion.

Compassion. Marisa seemed to come by it naturally. Look what she'd built here in Helena, by noticing the needs around her. What a difference she made for these single moms and their kids, not by giving them a handout, but by teaching them. Mentoring them. Befriending them.

He'd been such an idiot in Africa.

His saucer whooshed toward the snowman and the car that was turning into the driveway beyond. This thing had better speed than anything he'd ridden, but the ability to steer? Not so much.

The car. In that split second he recognized Avalon's Saab. He rolled off the saucer an instant before he would have hit the snowman. The disk shot toward the car. Avalon slammed her brakes as plastic crunched under her tires.

Jase winced. Not only from the pain in his shoulder from hitting the ground so hard, but also from the pain of seeing some unknown child's sled get totaled. The car, horn blaring, slid sideways before coming to a complete stop inches from the greenhouse.

He heaved himself upright using the snowman for support then ran to make sure she was okay. He only made two steps before hitting the hard-packed driveway. His boots shot out from underneath him and he sprawled for the second time.

Oh, the indignity. He lay still for a moment, stunned, then rolled over to his knees. First steps first.

Baxter licked his face. Ew.

"You okay, Jase?" Concern laced Marisa's words as she came alongside him.

He pulled himself upright with a strong grip on her hand then leaned on her for support, rubbing his hip with his sore arm. "Yeah, I'm going to live. Pretty sure, anyway."

The driver's door swung open and Avalon emerged, clad in a long sable coat and her favorite Sergio Rossi boots. Those high-heeled things had been made for dressing up, not walking on ice. She clutched the side of her car as she edged toward him and Marisa.

Under his arm, Marisa stiffened. Apparently she hadn't recognized the vehicle as it pulled in. Jase leaned closer and whispered, "I didn't know she was coming. Honest."

"How did she even know you were here?" Marisa's eyes shot daggers.

Uh.

Marisa pulled away from his hold, and he grabbed at the snowman for support. She had no such worries as she strode toward Avalon's car. Whatever soles her boots had, he needed some of those.

"Hi, Avalon. Wow, that was a close call. Can I help you with something?" Her tone was pleasant enough on the surface, but chilly enough to drop the air's temperature to single digits.

Oh man. Just what he needed.

Kristen, Charlotte, and Lila bailed off their tube a few feet away.

Avalon's eyes gleamed in satisfaction. "Well, this looks like a lovely little party. Thanks for letting me know, Jase."

He *what*? He hadn't told her.

Avalon minced over to Jase, somehow remaining

upright. "Sorry I'm late, Jase darling. I spoke with Daddy and assured him we'd just had a temporary misunderstanding. He'll reconsider on the other little issue he spoke with you about."

Jase stared at her, tightening his grip on the snowman's head. He slid from lack of support, the snowball rolling off and smashing at his feet. The body fell and broke into several pieces as he struggled to stay upright, his hip still painful from his first fall.

Avalon slid under his flailing arm and he clutched at her. "There, Jase. It's all right."

Marisa stood with hands on both hips. Glaring at *him*? "You wrecked the kids' snowman."

"I didn't mean to." He removed his arm from Avalon, who snickered but kept hers in place.

"You'd think I'd be a quicker learner." Marisa's gaze pierced his a moment longer then she turned and held out her hands to the two little girls who stood frozen nearby. "Come. Let's get some hot cocoa."

Baxter whined and trotted off.

"Are there gingerbread man cookies?" Charlotte tugged Marisa toward the house.

"Even better," said Lila. "Gingerbread angels. They're yummy."

"Sure." Marisa kicked the carrot out of her way and glanced at him over her shoulder. "Let's get some."

He barely caught the next words, mumbled under her breath. "While Avalon and Jase see themselves out."

His heart joined his shoulder and hip in throbbing pain.

CHAPTER 11

*A*re you trying to tell me if I eat like you..." The woman scowled at the sash across Marisa's chest proclaiming her Miss Tomah CSA. "I'll be beautiful like you? I don't think so."

The camera-ready smile froze on Marisa's face. "No, that's not what I'm saying at all." Why did some people hate what they didn't have? This frazzled woman would likely find a measure of tranquility watching a garden grow, and the bored young ones in tow might find it fascinating as well. Anyone would be more attractive if she were contented and at peace.

"That organic label is some made-up thing so food will cost more. There's nothing to it. What ordinary people can afford stuff like that?"

Marisa thought of her young mom friends. For many of them, gardening was the best first step toward serving the healthiest food possible. She softened her gaze at the woman in front of her. "There are ways nearly every family can afford real food. Most things are cheaper if you do them yourself, so a good step for many people is to grow a garden. And the other way is to choose basic foods from the outside edges of your supermarket — meat, dairy, and produce — and avoid the convenience packages in the middle. Paying someone else to prepare food for us adds to the cost."

"Who's got time for all that? Not in this day and age."

One of the kids tugged at her arm. "Mama, I want a burger and fries. You said we could get some after that boring place." He dragged out the word boring as though the magnificent State Capitol with its gold inlays, stained-glass windows, and domed ceilings was a drafty shack.

Marisa reached out to the woman but pulled back before touching her. "Like that. A pound of beef and the rest of the fixings cost so much less at the grocery store than even the cheapest fast food place, and you control what else goes in." She wasn't even going to start with the anti-GMO talk or the horrors of feedlots.

The woman rolled her eyes. "You're crazy. You haven't done a day's work in your life."

She shouldn't allow herself to be pulled into this discussion with the other contestants arrayed around her, to say nothing of Jase. They'd just arrived for a tour of the Capitol, with photo opportunities set up with various state and local politicians.

Marisa played with the flared hem of her fitted coral top over its matching pencil skirt. She'd freeze to death in the biting December wind if they didn't get inside quickly. But she couldn't resist. "We have programs out at Hiller Farm for families interested in learning about food. Look us up online, and be in touch. I'd love to discuss it more with you another time."

The woman shook her head. "You make it sound like you're a farmer yourself. As though you'd ever get dirt under your fingernails."

Marisa happened to know her nails were perfect today, but that they always looked this way was laughable. She opened her mouth to respond, but the woman turned to a contestant behind Marisa.

"You're raising money for breast cancer research? Bless you. My mother died of that horrible disease."

As Avalon reached forward to shake the woman's hand, her elbow caught Marisa's arm. No way was that an accident. "Thank you. It's time we found a cure."

No argument from Marisa. But food was important, too. In fact, evidence mounted that real food helped prevent cancer of all kinds.

"At least you're talking about something useful." The woman cast a cutting glare at Marisa before turning back to Avalon. "I hope you win."

"I hope so, too. I appreciate your kind words." A smirk played around Avalon's mouth as she focused on the woman.

"Mama, you promised!"

"Yes, yes, I'm coming." She turned from the contestants to swoop her brood past Thomas Meagher's horse statue and down the sidewalk.

"So how did that feel?" Avalon murmured for Marisa's ears alone. "I thought it felt pretty good, myself."

Marisa didn't deign to reply or even let Avalon know

she'd heard. She stepped forward, rubbing her exposed arms as though she could smooth the goose bumps.

Kristen bustled up from the back of the group. "Let's carry on, then. Move ahead, everyone." She led the way to the steps of the Capitol as she jabbered about the agenda for the afternoon's excursion. "Let's get a few quick shots on the steps before we head inside."

A grin cracked Marisa's face. Jase hated those words. To him, there was no such thing as a few quick shots. Not when every person needed to be carefully placed, the lighting checked, the background analyzed. For all she knew, he tested the angle of the wind like a pilot.

But no argument from her. When they'd shot beach-wear on location, she'd often thought she'd melt into a puddle of goo in the tropical sun. Her job wasn't to think about the weather, but to pose as requested and do her best.

Still, by the time they'd finally entered the relative warmth of the Capitol, she could all but see the frostbite creeping across her skin. Her toes had frozen inside her coral pumps, and her silk stockings hadn't done much to protect her legs.

"I thought we were going to freeze to death out there," Diana Riley murmured to Marisa.

"I'm sorry about engaging the woman," Marisa whispered back. The exchange hadn't taken long, but still.

"Don't worry about it. There's always someone around who shuns pageantry because they don't understand it." Diana nudged Marisa's arm. "But that was a new tactic, even so."

It was hard to be amused. Instead, Marisa turned to

survey the magnificent structure. She hadn't been here since high school. Had it been her government class that had done a tour? She couldn't even remember.

Looking up into the dome several stories up, she caught her breath. The deep coral on the massive corner walls supporting the stained glass rotunda was an intense version of her outfit. And oh, the gold inlaid everywhere on the arches, the walls, the ceilings. Everywhere she looked, magnificence.

"Amazing," Jase breathed at her elbow.

Startled, she shifted away from him. "It is, isn't it? I'd forgotten the treasure we have right here."

"It rivals anyplace on the East coast." He swiveled slowly, eyes trained upward. "Maybe not the European cathedrals."

Was that a glimmer of longing she heard in his voice? A lilt that spoke of dreaming about travel? A dream they'd once shared. She'd thought hers satisfied as she'd made a home on the farm, but the pageant — and Jase — had brought it all back like a tsunami.

Or like an avalanche of snow. Remembering the doomed tobogganing party, she took another step away.

He didn't seem to notice but grinned at her, a shadow lingering in the back of his eyes. "But who needs them, right? When there's something this grand right here in our own backyard?"

He meant to stay in Helena, then. Back when she'd dreamed of life with Jase, it hadn't included more than random visits home to Montana. But those dreams were in the past. She'd been younger then. More impressionable. How could she entertain thoughts of him now, when her own restlessness grew again? She couldn't. There was Avalon to consider, too. For all Jase's sweet words to Marisa, Avalon had some appeal to him as well.

She stepped to the other side of Diana, who commented on the wide marble steps leading up to a gigantic half-circle stained glass window.

An older man garbed in the green golf shirt of the Montana Historical Society approached the group. He rubbed his hands together as he surveyed them. "Hi. I'm Joe, your guide today." He started into his spiel as they ascended the staircase.

A man in a three-piece suit rounded the corner above them and began his descent. It took Marisa an instant to place him as her stockbroker, Mr. Penhaven.

Her breath caught. Mr. Penhaven? She glanced at Avalon, a few steps behind and over by the marble balustrade. He couldn't be. No. Not the man who—?

"Daddy? How good to see you."

He could. The man with whom she'd entrusted her savings for Bren's kids was Avalon's father.

JASE STIFLED A GROAN. No matter where he went, Avalon's father seemed to be there. It wasn't his place to keep Avalon focused on the event at hand. If anyone needed to intervene, it would be Kristen, not him. He feigned fascination with the painting at the head of the stairs, not hard to do. The Last Spike? For a fleeting moment he tried to imagine the huge boon the railway had been to the West in 1883.

But it was not to be.

"Jase, my boy." Mr. Penhaven's jovial voice broke through Jase's studious examination of the stained-glass canopy above the grand staircase.

In that instant Jase saw not only Avalon's smug expression, but Marisa's one of horror. But why? How could she know Avalon's father? She couldn't think he had romantic feelings left for Avalon. Not after what he'd said to her in the cathedral.

But at the sledding party, when Marisa had all but accused him of breaking the kids' snowman on purpose, she'd been reacting to Avalon more than him, right? But she still hadn't accepted his phone calls of apology. Wait. What had Avalon said there?

Something about Daddy.

Who stood here in front of Jase at the moment, expression narrowing by the second as Jase failed to respond. He pulled a smile to his face, hoping it reflected in his eyes, doubting that it did. "Hi, Mr. Penhaven."

What was the man doing in the Capitol? His investment offices were in the building he owned in Last Chance Gulch, right upstairs from Jase's.

From the corner of his eye, Jase watched Marisa's coral outfit turn right into the corridor at the top of the staircase. She stood beside Diana Riley, both gazing up at the stained-glass canopy. In the distance, Joe droned on about the history of the building.

"Of all the beautiful women I see you're here with the most beautiful of them all." Mr. Penhaven's eyes watch Jase closely. "Good choice."

Presumably he meant Avalon. "This truly is a group of talented and gorgeous women. No doubt about it."

"Young guys like you hunger after them, don't you? But all you need is one." Mr. Penhaven's hand rested on Avalon's shoulder. "In fact, it seems rather unbecoming of you to take photos of so many women. Probably some of them were barely wearing anything at all when you did so."

Jase's temper began to rise. "Not true, sir. Sure, I've done swimwear sessions, but that's definitely the limit for me. I've lost a few contracts because of it, but I stand firm to my convictions."

"A talented photographer like you must do well in family portraits, or perhaps landscapes."

Was the guy for real? "The money's in modeling. I've had a break, but I'm thinking of getting back into it." If only to get away from the Penhaven family. What of Marisa? Maybe he could convince her to come along. Maybe she missed her modeling days, too.

His heart sank. Everything she did proved her devotion to her mother, the CSA, the families she helped through the farm. Not a chance of her going anywhere.

But how could he convince Avalon and her father to leave him alone if he stayed?

He stared Mr. Penhaven in the eye as he climbed two steps, finally able to look down on the older man. "Excuse me, sir. My work is waiting for me. I'm on the clock."

Whether Avalon followed him or not, he didn't care. He took the steps two at a time and rejoined the group by the bronze statues below the rotunda. He angled himself toward Marisa, but she sidled closer to the center of the group.

Jase took a deep breath and slowly released it. He couldn't convince Marisa of his intentions so long as the Penhavens stalked him. And that's exactly what it felt like. He did the only thing he could think of, and breathed a prayer to his Heavenly Father, asking for wisdom and patience. Asking for another chance. A real chance with Marisa. He couldn't let her go again.

He opened his eyes as he felt a whisper of air at his elbow.

Avalon smirked up at him.

CHAPTER 12

"Whoa, girl. You look more African than I do."

Marisa grinned at Diana, who poked her head into the tiny bathroom. The two girls shared a room in the historic Tomah House on the grounds of the Grizzly Gulch Resort.

"Not so much on skin color." Marisa adjusted the vibrantly colored beaded piece lying heavily on her shoulders.

"Or hair. You could do the thousands-of-braids look."

Marisa laughed. "With what for time? I'd need ten hairdressers to get it done in time for the evening gown competition."

Diana tilted her head. "That's a Masai collar, right? I think those women shave their heads at the drop of a hat." A gleam formed in her eyes. "That would be faster than braiding."

"Nice try." Marisa twirled in the small space. "What do you think?"

Her roommate gave her the once-over.

The bold red single-shoulder gown was also a nod to the Masai, but the lines were more flattering than the traditional dresses.

"You can sure pull it off. But I don't get why. If you've got a drop of African blood in you, it's well hidden."

"Have you ever been to Africa?" Marisa edged out to give Diana space for preparation.

Diana leaned in close to the mirror, examining her complexion. "Can't say that I have. You?"

"Twice. South Africa and Kenya."

"Hence the Masai?"

Marisa nodded. "On a photo shoot a few years ago, we spent a couple of days in Nairobi relaxing after an intensive week on the beach at Mombasa." Days immersed in a new relationship with Jase, with whom she'd been on several shoots over the previous six months. Days dreaming of what delights the future might hold. "I have friends who do mission work there, with the Masai."

How he'd react to her choice of formal gown tonight would be very telling. When she'd planned her wardrobe for pageant week, it had seemed like they might pick up their relationship from those days. Forgive and forget and all that. But with Avalon... it was hard to know. Hard to trust him.

She didn't really know what he wanted. Maybe he didn't either, but there would be time to sort that all out after the pageant.

Win or lose.

But she was counting on winning. Counting on something new — something challenging — to occupy her for a year. She'd always thrived on change, and she'd grown vegetables in one plot of ground for three summers.

"Well, the red looks good on you, and that necklace thing makes quite a statement, especially with the belt."

"Oh, I forgot the earrings." Marisa reached into her jewelry box and pulled out a pair of hoops beaded to match. Angling the stand mirror on the desk, she put them into place. She swung her head from side to side, admiring her reflection as the three-inch circles whirled.

Diana appeared, now clothed in a glittering gold gown with turquoise accents.

Marisa whistled. "Wow, you are stunning!"

"You like?" Diana pirouetted.

"Amazing. Really. No one would ever guess you were a lawyer."

Diana chuckled. "I'm not sure if that's a compliment or not."

Marisa laughed with her. "I'm not sure, either."

"Are you a praying person?" Diana turned, halfway to the door.

"Yes." Though she'd been too busy to spend the time lately that her soul craved. Marisa closed her eyes for an instant, gathering strength. "You?"

"Would you mind if we prayed together before going over to the event center?"

"I'd be delighted."

As Diana's words of praise and adoration for their Lord washed over Marisa, peace settled in. Had she not asked for God's will before entering and given the results of the pageant over to Him? Had she not placed her relationship with Jase in those same capable hands? She had. Thousands of times.

Now it was a thousand and one.

IT FELT good to dig in and work long, intensive days again. Almost like shooting on location. Jase double-checked that he had several empty SD cards tucked into the specialty wallet in his pocket. Shots from the Capitol had already been downloaded and sorted. He'd even emailed several in for tomorrow's paper, limiting himself to one of Marisa.

He was as ready for the evening gown competition as he was going to be. At least until his thoughts drifted to Marisa. Then he only hoped he'd remember to document the rest of the evening, too. Not just her.

The door opened and Kristen poked her head around it. "Ready?"

"Yes, ma'am."

His sister grinned. "And don't forget to keep up that tone of respect, little brother. We've got under an hour until the event begins, so you'll have to shoot fast."

Jase waved his hand at her. "Get rolling then. I'm a pro. It won't be my fault if you're late."

She wrinkled up her nose at him and ducked out of sight. A moment later Avalon strolled in. Glam girl.

"Over here, Avalon." He pointed her to the prepared set. "We've got about three minutes. Ready?"

For once she gave him the professional attention he needed to get his job done and, in no time, Diana Riley took Avalon's place.

Every time the door opened, Jase's pulse sped up. Then, when someone other than Marisa entered, he settled into his job. Each woman was beautiful. Each deserved his best work, his attention to detail. But sooner or later, it would be her.

Number twenty. Marisa swished into the room.

He wasn't prepared for her. Not by a long shot. His gaze riveted on the Masai collar resting on her bare shoulder. In a heartbeat, he was in Nairobi. The group of African women marched down the street. The raucous vendors called their wares above the ever-present music. The smells of spicy biriyani mingled with less pleasant odors. Colors swirled like a kaleidoscope, Masai red forming the ground for all the rest.

Jase blinked.

Only one woman stood before him. Yes, clothed in a single-shouldered red dress with a nod to the Masai styling. Yes, with the vibrant, multi-beaded collar, belt and — now that he looked closer — earrings.

But Marisa Hiller didn't belong to Africa. She belonged to Helena. Did she — could she possibly — have a foot on each continent, as he sometimes felt he did?

Could she belong to him?

He gave his head a quick shake. Not in the sense of ownership. But as a partnership. A team.

"Jase?"

"You look amazing. Masai?" Not that there was a question. Those days were permanently etched, not only in the backs of his eyelids, but on the very core of his being.

"Yes." She turned, the vibrant red gown swirling around her ankles. "Like it?" She met his gaze.

"Very much." He could drown in those brown eyes. "Marisa, I—"

She strode the few steps to the center of his backdrop. "Here?"

Right. His camera. His job. The Miss Snowflake Pageant. He could see her with the tiara on her dark hair. Holding a gauze veil in place. Her dress shimmered into white.

The confused expression on her face pulled him back to reality yet again. He lifted the camera, cherishing the moment he could feast his eyes on her. Capture her exquisite beauty.

He clicked the camera one last time and lowered it. He filled his eyes with all the begging he could muster. "Marisa, we need to talk."

From outside the room, a buzzer sounded.

Marisa's focus slipped to the door before resting back on him.

Jase took a step closer, then another. He could feel the warmth radiating from her body. Smell the subtle perfume she wore. Not Masai. All Marisa.

This wasn't the time, wasn't the place, but he couldn't help himself any more than he could stop the clock from ticking.

He reached for her shoulders. "I love you," he whispered, losing himself in the bottomless brown eyes fixed on his and the sensation of her silken skin beneath his hands.

The studio door flung open, and the cacophony from the banquet hall beyond blurted into the little room.

"Ready?" Kristen's voice topped the babble. "Oops. Hey, you two. No time for mushy stuff."

If it were just about him, he'd shut that door firmly on his sister's face. But it wasn't about him. It was about Marisa and her chance to win the Miss Snowflake title. He brushed his lips across her forehead and tugged her closer for a quick hug. "Go get 'em." He released her, his arms cold and empty.

Marisa's eyes held wonder as she glanced at Kristen then back to him. "Thanks," she murmured, and was gone.

Kristen winked and pulled the door shut behind Marisa, leaving Jase to collect his gear and his composure before heading to the banquet hall.

Had he been gentle enough? Had she welcomed him? He closed his eyes, the taste of her skin fresh on his lips.

Please, Lord.

THE EVENING gown competition blurred past Marisa, no matter how she forced her attention to lock onto the evening's emcee and to do her part.

Jase looked so much like his dad must have thirty years ago. The senior Mackie's gray hair still carried a shot of red. William spoke with composure from the podium, a voice so like Jase's that if Marisa had closed her eyes, she might've been pulled into it. His lithe build, his straightforward gaze, his ready laugh — all reminiscent of his son.

How could Jase turn out badly if he were so like his father? He couldn't.

She found Jase's mother at a nearby table, an elegant woman with a quick smile for the two small grandchildren wiggling on chairs between her and her son-in-law. Kristen slipped into the empty seat beside Todd. He leaned over and kissed her on the cheek, leaving his arm draped across the back of her chair when he refocused on Dr. Mackie.

Marisa's forehead warmed where Jase's lips had brushed her a half-hour before. Heard again his whispered words of love. She could have what Kristen had in Todd. A strong marriage. Adorable kids. Supportive in-laws.

The assembly clapped as William stepped away from the mic. For an instant Marisa's disorientation grew. She'd already given her speech, hadn't she? Hadn't all of them done so?

A vague memory surfaced. Yes. Definitely tonight, the end of the first full day of competition. She'd done well. The camera flashes had kept up their blazing throughout. Not just Jase's but others. Reporters, maybe. People had clapped.

Around her, the other contestants stood then joined friends and family members off-stage. The buzz of voices grew, punctuated by laughter and the clink of glasses. She should probably find Mom and Bob. They were here somewhere. Toward the back.

A touch on her arm brought Marisa's thoughts into focus. She turned as Kristen slipped into the chair next to her and leaned close.

"I didn't have a chance to tell you before the banquet, but I absolutely love your outfit tonight. Amazing nod to the Masai."

"You recognized it?" Marisa hadn't been surprised that Diana had... and even less that Jase had. But others?

"Oh, yes. Jase has shown us so many pictures of his trips to Kenya and Tanzania."

Marisa's brain reeled. "His what?"

Kristen touched the beaded collar with a gentle finger. "This is gorgeous. Jase brought a little one for Charlotte, but I didn't know what to pair it with on her. Now I wish he'd given me one, too."

"I'm sorry. Did you just say he'd been to Africa many times?"

Kristen's green eyes looked deep into Marisa's. "Wow, you guys need to talk."

Jase's words. Apparently correct. But she wouldn't let her eyes go hunting for him right now. "What was he doing in Africa?" Even as she asked, Marisa knew the answer. Just because she'd left the business right away didn't mean he had. "More fashion shoots, I imagine."

"One or two, I think. But no. That's not what he showed us pictures of. Those were from the time he went to help make the documentary."

The room contained very little air. "The what?"

"The documentary about mission work with the Masai. Didn't he tell you about that?"

CHAPTER 13

The gallery space was too small for twenty Christmas trees. Maybe it would be easier to move around once all the contestants and their helpers had completed their decorating tasks. The babble of dozens of women roiled past Marisa as she paused in the doorway, and the overpowering scent of as many kinds of perfume assaulted her senses.

Marisa peered over the boxes of garden-themed ornaments and garlands in her arms then stepped into the room as Kristen breezed over.

"Hi, Marisa! I was hoping you'd get here soon." She pointed to the back corner of the space, where a lone fir tree stood in its stand, away from the bustle of activity.

"Over there, eh?" Bob elbowed past them both and set his boxes on the floor beside the tree. He dumped his jacket beside the boxes and hitched his pants. "What do you want me to do first?"

The room stilled. Without turning, Marisa knew all eyes in the room were focused their way. Okay, she wouldn't have picked Bob out of a lineup as her decorating helper, but he was the only volunteer. Mom's charity board meeting was this morning, and she was vice president. She couldn't really skip.

And, well, Bob was eager to help. Who knew? He might even have a good idea or two.

"First, the lights." Marisa set her load down beside Bob's and glanced around the room.

The noise level picked up as the other contestants stopped staring and resumed work on their own trees. Nearly every conifer in the room already shimmered with white twinkle lights.

Hers would, too, but once they were up, nothing about her tree would look like anyone else's. She wanted to win this segment of the pageant, and it was open to voting from the public. People might love her tree or hate it, but they'd notice it. They'd remember it. They'd talk about it.

With Bob's help, she began winding light strands around her tree.

It was going to be the most unique tree in the gallery.

JASE PAUSED in the doorway to the gallery space in Mr. Penhaven's building on Last Chance Gulch. The place was alive with activity — rather a lot of activity for the size of the room.

"Jase, darling." Avalon's sweet words didn't reach her eyes. Her gaze narrowed slightly as she spoke.

"Hi, Avalon." Of course her tree was one of the two

nestled closest to the window. She'd either arrived first, or Daddy had staked out her spot for her. Possibly both.

Avalon's mother approached Jase and cradled his face between her palms before he could step back out of reach. She kissed the air on both sides. "Jase. So good to see you."

Great. There went unbiased-photographer status. But he had to be polite, and he had to start somewhere. "Hi, Mrs. Penhaven. I'm here to take some in-progress photos. Want to tell me about Avalon's tree?"

The woman launched into a description of every item hanging from the branches. Thankfully sparseness was a decorating decision they'd made, so he didn't have to smile and nod for long after snapping a few shots.

He moved to the next tree, decorated with valentines for heart health, and listened while Diana Riley explained her choices.

Tabitha Jensen's tree was liberally sprinkled with fake snow and adorned with snowflakes. It had little to do with the children's charity she sponsored, but it was pretty.

Another contestant's tree celebrated habitat for humanity with dozens of tiny house ornaments and a garland of nails.

This trees for charities idea of his dad's had been genius. But Jase knew he was getting closer and closer to Marisa's fir. Somehow she'd landed in the back corner, but that wouldn't matter to the public. The glitz in the front window might pull them into the gallery but once inside, each tree would be given its own chance for the winning votes.

Marisa did everything with class. Her tree would reflect it, no doubt. He cast a quick glance in her direction, but several people blocked his view of her project. Best to focus on one tree at a time, even though most of the contestants had to realize his heart had been captured by one of them. There was no way he'd leave space for anyone to challenge that his photography was anything less than completely fair.

A few minutes later he turned, and there it was. And yet, not at all what he'd expected. Dozens of blown-glass vegetables hung from the branches. Red tomatoes, golden corn, branches of broccoli, and deeply purple eggplants. But the crowning touch had to be the miles of pea-green beaded garland winding around and around the tree as a final nod to the CSA's veggie theme.

The grin on his face exploded into a chuckle.

Marisa narrowed her gaze at him.

"No, really, this is awesome. What a unique idea."

Bob stuck his thumbs through his jeans' belt loops. "Yep. We told her how we wanted this tree done. She was gonna do something ordinary until the CSA board got involved."

"It's like buried treasure." He caught Marisa's gaze and held tight. Treasure all right. This was one he wouldn't release. Not ever again, if he could only convince her that he'd changed.

"Vegetables?" Avalon slipped her hand into the crook of his arm. "What an interesting, if bucolic, idea."

Jase stepped away, managing to lose the physical contact. But the connection with Marisa was also gone.

"Broccoli, ma'am," said Bob.

Avalon stared down her nose at the short CSA director. "Pardon me?"

MORE THAN A TIARA

"It's pronounced broccoli. Not bucolly or whatever it is you said."

"I know what broccoli is, mister."

Jase bit his lip to keep from smirking. He'd bet his bottom dollar Bob knew what bucolic was, too.

Marisa smiled at Avalon. Quite gracious, really, though it didn't look like the good humor reached her eyes. "This was a fun tree to put together. Who knew vegetables were so popular with artisans, anyway?"

Avalon's nose twitched. "Who knew, indeed." She turned her back to Marisa and tucked her hand under Jase's elbow again. "Are you nearly done? We could get some lunch at the Mediterranean Grill before the doors open to the public here."

"No, thanks." Jase smiled to soften his words, but there was no way he was getting pulled in. Not when Marisa was right here listening in. Not even if she wasn't. In fact... "As soon as Marisa is done, she and I are grabbing a bite at The Parrot. And Bob, too, of course." No need to tell anyone he'd stashed a sandwich in his pocket, just in case she said no.

Avalon's thin eyebrows rose. "You're taking Bob on a date?"

Bob fussed with his jeans' waistband. "Yup. Brian makes the best chili."

"Well, good luck. All you need is a few beans to change the aroma in this gallery." In case he'd missed her meaning, Avalon's fingers fluttered past her nose for an instant.

But Jase's eyes slid straight past her to Marisa, eyeing him speculatively. Didn't matter. Bob agreed, and that was as good as a win with Marisa. Right?

Marisa set her spoon back in her nearly empty chili bowl. "When were you going to tell me about the Masai documentary?"

Jase's startled gaze met hers across the wooden booth. "The what?"

"Kristen told me." It'd been eating Marisa since last night. He'd apologized for his part in their fight in Africa. Why hadn't he gone the extra step and told her what he'd done to atone? Or maybe he hadn't meant it as redemption. If not, then what?

"Masai?" Bob wanted to know. "That's the African necklace thing you wore yesterday, right? Bold statement, that."

But Marisa didn't reply. Just waited for Jase to acknowledge her question. Come up with something. All this stalling had to be for some purpose.

"I went back a couple of times." He stared down at his hands, twisting the paper napkin into a tight roll. "To Kenya."

As though that had needed explanation. "And?"

"I wanted to see... needed to figure out what had caught your attention."

Swallowing became difficult. Did she even remember what it had all been about? Yes. Those hungry kids. Starving orphans begging on the streets. She wanted to help them, but a meal today would only help for a little while. They needed a food source they could come back to, like a garden. Food they could grow themselves in pots and vacant places. What could have been more important than providing the tools for these kids to feed themselves?

Jase hadn't seen that. He'd seen a model high on herself, drawing attention to the orphans to show the world how great she was. That hadn't been in her thoughts at all. How many nights had she wrestled that demon? Way too many.

Marisa set her jaw and stared at him across the table. If only Kenya had never happened. If only her memories of JFK were a bad dream. She could really fall for this guy if they didn't have such a painful history.

He glanced up then down. "You were right. I was wrong."

Bob cleared his throat. "Sounds like you kids need to talk, but they're opening the doors to the public in under five minutes."

Heat burned up Marisa's neck and flooded her cheeks. How had she forgotten Bob sitting beside her? She fumbled for her purse and flipped her hair over her shoulder. "Best be going then."

MARISA STRAIGHTENED her slanting tree in its stand. It had been perfectly vertical when she'd left for The Parrot, hadn't it? And the peas-in-a-pod garland drooped in places she was certain it hadn't. A swift glance toward Avalon beside her perfect tree by the main door showed an animated contestant speaking to a visitor.

Let it go. She couldn't prove anything. Nothing was broken. Nothing had been disrupted that she couldn't quickly straighten. She could only be thankful Avalon hadn't been alone in the gallery. No doubt if she had, some of the fragile glass ornaments would be broken. Accidentally, of course.

"Marisa! Your tree looks great." Kristen stepped into Marisa's field of vision. "So unique."

"Thanks." Marisa wrenched her gaze from Avalon and smiled at her friend. Imagine that. Jase's sister was her friend. "The folks from the CSA made all the decisions of what to buy for it. I think it turned out pretty well." Unique was a nice word for it, but hey, why not stand out? There was only so much of being like everyone else that she could handle. It had never been her way.

"What happens to the trees afterward?" she asked Kristen. "Are they being auctioned off for charity?"

Kristen grimaced and shook her head. "We thought about that, but the timing isn't the greatest with the voting ending on Christmas Eve. Everyone already has trees by that time, so why bid then? There's really no time even to fit in an auction that afternoon."

"I can see the problem. Too bad."

"So everyone needs to take time on the twenty-sixth to come box up their ornaments. I know it's busy, but it's the reality of having a Christmas pageant."

Marisa nodded. "That shouldn't be a problem." It would be just her and Mom at home. Unless Bob came by. Or how about Jase? "What happens to the trees themselves?"

Kristen stared at her blankly and gave a weak laugh. "I hadn't thought that far yet."

"If you don't have a better plan, why not let Bob come by and pick them up? He'd be happy to chip them for mulch, I'm sure."

"What a great idea."

Kristen turned away and, through the open doorway, Marisa watched Jase cross the walking mall as a little boy Davy's age tugged on his jacket. Jase immediately crouched to talk to the kid eye-to-eye. A moment later he dug into his coat pocket and pulled out something wrapped in plastic wrap. A sandwich? The little guy accepted it and beamed before scampering off.

Jase. Maybe he had changed. Really changed. Once this pageant was over, win or lose, she'd pin him down and get the whole story out of him. And find out where his heart lived now.

Only a few more days of insanity.

CHAPTER 14

She'd skied at Divide dozens — maybe hundreds — of times as a teen, but hadn't ever aspired to taking the sport further. Today's crisp air swirled with fluffy snowflakes as though God's feather pillow sported a hole. The fresh snow muffled the sounds of the hill. The chair lift clanged in the distance, and an occasional shout of glee echoed into the area near the lodge.

Even the twenty contestants seemed more subdued than usual. Maybe it was the lack of sleep and the go-go-go pressure of the pageant getting to everyone. Three more days. Marisa could endure three more days.

"I feel like an imposter."

Marisa glanced at her roommate. Kristen wasn't the only solid friend she'd made this week. Diana certainly counted as well. "How come?"

Diana flashed a grin. "I haven't skied a day in my life."

"Once the photo shoot is over, I'll take you to the top of the bunny hill and give you a lesson."

Diana stepped back and raised both hands in mock

horror. "Ha. No, you won't. We have our next event in just a few hours, and the bus won't wait."

"Come back next week and we'll do it then."

"So generous of you. But no. Even this great outfit from Capital Sports can't make me look like I belong up here."

"Because of your color?" Marisa had seen African-Americans on the slopes. Not many, in Montana, but certainly some.

Diana wrinkled her nose. "No, silly. Because it takes more than playing dress-up to make someone into something she's not."

"Sounds like it won't be much consolation, but the lime green ski jacket really pops off your complexion."

"I hate to say it, but you are practically camouflaged in that white." Diana winked. "And not because of your skin color, either."

Marisa laughed. "Too true. My sponsor didn't think about the fact there'd be nothing but snow up here. Go figure. It's a ski hill, right? They should be hoping for snow."

Sure, she'd had a bit of say in which outfit had been loaned her. Normally all white wouldn't have been her choice, but the blazing purple scarf and mitts had sucked her into it.

"Over here, everyone!" Kristen called out. "Set your coffee and snacks down on the table and let's get some group shots before going to individuals."

Marisa shifted away from the table as several of the girls approached with Styrofoam cups and protein bars. She took one last sip of her mocha just as something rammed into her back.

Hot brown liquid sloshed down the front of her white ski jacket. She stared, frozen in time, as rivulets drizzled down.

"Hey, be more careful!" Diana's voice rang out. She pressed a stack of paper napkins into Marisa's hand.

"Oh, I'm dreadfully sorry."

Avalon? Marisa should have known.

"You stepped back into my path as I was about to go around you."

Great. She probably had a coffee splash down her back to match the front.

"Didn't look like it to me," Diana growled. "Your elbow swung out to get her in the back."

"I slipped on the ice." Avalon peered at the front of Marisa's jacket. "I'm so sorry. I do hope that won't stain."

Did anyone besides her and Diana hear the falseness in Avalon's voice? Marisa bit back all the things she really wanted to say. What was more important? Looking good in front of the group? Teaching Avalon a lesson? Or keeping her cool and allowing God to decide the outcome?

I choose door number three.

Barely. Marisa smiled at Avalon, trying to make it a real smile. "I hope it doesn't stain, either." Because it looked like she'd just bought herself an expensive white ski outfit. Really practical for someone who rarely skied and who dreamed of returning to African soil.

Avalon smirked and set her cup on the table before strutting away to the group rendezvous area.

Diana stared after her. "She did that on purpose."

Paper napkins were no match for a splash of mocha on a

white jacket, even with a handful of snow to try to dilute the stain. "Maybe," Marisa allowed.

"Maybe? She's out-of-control jealous of you. Everything you say or do, she belittles."

If Diana only knew. Marisa clenched her jaw. No, she wasn't going there.

"Diana? Marisa? We're waiting," Kristen called.

Marisa turned to the gathering group and held her head up high, daring anyone to comment. From the back row, Avalon smirked and brushed her streaked blond hair over her shoulder. Perfectly put together, as always.

Gasps came from the group. Tabitha's hand flew up to cover her mouth, and she wasn't the only one.

"Oh, no! What happened?" Kristen strode closer, but she slipped on the ice and her feet shot out from under her, clipboard and pen flying in different directions.

Marisa gritted her teeth against blurting out, "Avalon happened." Even though it was true, it wasn't in her best interests to announce it. "It was an accident."

Diana muffled a snort as she picked up Kristen's scattered implements.

"Are you okay?" Marisa helped Kristen back to her feet. "That looks like it must've hurt."

Kristen rubbed her backside. "Nothing wounded but my pride." She glanced over her shoulder at the waiting group then lowered her voice. "You?"

Marisa held her friend's gaze. "Same. I can't believe I was that clumsy." Or dumb enough to let Avalon get behind her without noticing.

"I can't believe it, either." Kristen raised her eyebrows.

Marisa shook her head slightly. So not going there. "If you stick me in the back row, the stain won't show."

"Sure, find a spot. We'll figure out something for the individual shots."

Jase. She'd nearly forgotten about him. Marisa raised her chin a little. If he backed away from her because of the clumsy story then he wasn't worth wasting her dreams on.

And, exhausted as she was every single night of this competition, her dreams took her to the Kenyan beach every time she lay down. They stood, bare toes burrowed in the warm sand, a sea-laden breeze wafting over them. She felt his arms around her, holding her close, and the soft cotton of his favorite casual shirt under her arms and cheek. His kisses on her hair, her forehead. Her lips.

She blinked.

Jase stood in front of her.

HE'D SEEN the whole thing from fifty feet away, where he'd been talking to one of the guys from the ski rental shop, from the smirk on Avalon's face as she came up behind Marisa clear through to the end result.

And Marisa said she'd been clumsy? That it had been an accident? Not a chance.

He looked deep into her eyes, his mouth open to announce what he'd seen.

Kristen put a hand on his arm. "Time to start taking photos, Jase. We've got less than two hours before the bus returns us to Helena."

"But—"

"We'll deal with this later."

He glanced at his sister and back at Marisa. "But that snowsuit is ruined, and it was no accident."

"I know it. You know it. Marisa knows it. But we don't have time."

"Can you kick Avalon out of competition?"

Marisa's cheeks blanched.

Kristen's grip on his arm tightened. "Jason Mackie, your job is to take photos. Now get over there and finish setting up."

The little brother in him surged up a desire to rebel, but the expression on Marisa's face stopped him cold. "This isn't over." He turned toward the table holding his camera gear. Good thing no one had dumped coffee on it.

Marisa joined the waiting group while Kristen consulted her clipboard and Jase checked his light meter and took a few test shots.

"Ready?"

The women nodded and smiled. A few called out an affirmative.

"Let's get started." By shifting half a step to his left, Diana's shoulder blocked the stain on Marisa's jacket. No problem. If anything showed when he zoomed in, he'd edit it out. The public would never know what happened.

A few minutes later, he started on the individuals. Somehow Avalon moved to the front of the line in her caramel-colored outfit. She smiled sweetly at him, her eyes glimmering behind the mascara.

Once he'd thought that look was reserved for him. That it meant some kind of affection. Now he recognized it as the expression reserved for when she was smugly proud of herself.

With Kristen at his elbow, he couldn't trust himself to say anything to Avalon beyond the requirements to get her photos done.

She pirouetted, gave him saucy grins, fluttered her eyelashes, and tossed him more than one coy look.

If she thought that's all it would take to lure him in, she had another think coming. A whole bunch of more thinks.

Jase dismissed her with a curt nod and glanced to see who was next, but a hand on his sleeve stilled him. He turned back to see Avalon with a wistful smile, as though he were simply blind to her charms. She didn't have any. It wasn't that he was blind to them. "Yes?"

She leaned in closer and pressed her lips to his.

Jase stumbled back then fixed her with a glare. "That was uncalled for."

Avalon winked, blew him another one, and sashayed away.

"She's got a lot of gall," Kristen said. "I don't mean to make it sound like no one could be attracted to you, little brother, but why is she so fixated?"

"You're the one who said we didn't have time for this."

"Right." Kristen turned to the women. "Heather? You're next."

Jase shifted into the zone as he worked through the next eighteen contestants. Finally Marisa stood before him.

He took a deep breath and let it out slowly. She exuded true beauty. Honest beauty. With blinding clarity, he realized this was the woman he wanted to wake up beside every morning for the rest of his life, no matter whether that was here in Helena or anywhere in the world. Nothing else mattered. Only her.

"I figured we could drape the scarf over the stain," Kristen said, fussing with the knitted purple length looped around Marisa's shoulders.

Marisa's eyes pulled away from his. As reluctantly as he did? The air felt chillier without her gaze holding his.

"I don't know, Kristen. It seems an awkward angle." Marisa fingered the scarf.

The coral turtleneck peeking from behind the zipper gave Jase an idea. "Why not open the jacket all the way? I think that will do it."

Kristen frowned. "It's freezing. Can't you edit the stain out?"

"Well, yes." Gladly, but he'd rather not have to. Every single day was packed. He was lucky to get four hours in bed after he'd tweaked and posted the best of the day's photos. And then it would be useful if he actually spent those four hours sleeping. No such luck, most nights. Not with Marisa dancing in his dreams.

She slid the zipper tab down and allowed Kristen to arrange and rearrange her turtleneck and the scarf.

Finally Kristen stepped back. "What do you think, Jase? Can you work with this?"

With the jacket artfully open and the scarf casually knotted, no trace of the mocha stain was evident. At least if he was careful of the angle — and he would be.

He raised the camera and took the first few shots, but Marisa's confidence seemed to have vanished.

Kristen called the other girls to attention and began

herding them to the bus waiting on the other side of the lodge.

Jase didn't dare look up to see what Avalon thought of Marisa lingering, but he wasn't finished with her. For one thing, she hadn't tossed him a genuine smile yet. He moved to the side, forcing a different angle.

The stain showed. He stepped closer and reached for the jacket lapel. "Mind if I rearrange this a little?"

Her hand gripped his.

Jase stilled. So close he could smell the floral scent of her. Feel the warmth from her body. He met her gaze and nearly drowned in the deep brown depths. "Marisa."

"I saw you yesterday. Did you give a sandwich to the little boy?"

It took a moment for his mind to catch up. He tried to break eye contact but it was impossible. "Yes."

"Didn't you think someone might see you do a good deed?" A slightly bitter sound tinged her words.

"Should I have let him go hungry instead, when I had the means to feed him?"

She leaned closer. Mere inches separated her face from his. "Should *I* have?"

Jase turned his hand to capture hers, both pressed in the tiny space between them. "No. You should have done everything you could to help, whether people were watching or not. Children should not go hungry. Not here in Helena or in Kenya if we have the ability to feed them."

He couldn't help himself but closed the gap between them with a soft kiss on her lips. He groaned as he pulled away. "Marisa. Whatever it takes. Wherever it goes, my life isn't complete without you."

Marisa's eyes searched his. "What if I tell you my motives weren't completely pure? Yes, I absolutely wanted to help the children grow food, but I wanted to be in the pictures, too. I didn't ask you to take photos of only them but of me with them."

He stroked her hair with his free hand. This moment was worth everything. "That didn't make your motives wrong, Marisa. Your connections — your face — could do what mere photos of hungry orphans could not do alone."

She blinked, still focused on him.

"I'm sorry my attention has made you Avalon's target, but I know what true love is. It's what I have for you."

Her gaze softened. Would she be able to let go of the past and let true love find her?

CHAPTER 15

*Y*ou keep saying, 'for the children,' Miss Tomah CSA. Yet children's needs aren't met with your organic food box program. That's only for the wealthy." The judge at the end of the panel flipped her pen over and over while watching Marisa over her glasses.

Marisa stood in the spotlight with an array of seven judges seated at a long table before her. Thank goodness for public speaking classes in college. She hadn't used the skills in years, as no one wanted to hear a model's opinions. Her job had been to pose and show the requested attitude.

Both were still a good idea. Marisa smiled at the judge. "There are children in every socio-economic group from pure poverty to extreme wealth. Children don't choose which woman they're born to. They can't pick to have a loving father and extended family. They can't even choose whether or not their mother keeps them. They can't choose if they're born in a ghetto or to a wealthy Rockefeller."

The judge raised her eyebrows. The pen kept rotating.

"All children deserve quality food in enough quantity to

thrive, not merely survive. Cooperatives across the country — around the world, really — like the Tomah Community Supported Agriculture program make this ideal much more possible for those with disposable income. That is very true."

The woman leaned back a little, a smug smile lurking at the corners of her mouth.

Marisa raised her hand and inhaled a prayer. This was what she detested. Using herself as a positive example. Laying some claim to being in the limelight. Jase's words yesterday lifted her up. "I'm not just the spokesperson for the Tomah CSA. I'm a farmer. My mother and I grow a wide variety of vegetables that are sold through the box program, but this enables us to use the remainder of our twenty acres for other purposes. This past summer five low-income single moms grew gardens on our property."

By golly, she was proud of that. Her voice rose in confidence. "Their children join them on the farm. Together these families are learning about the value of good nutrition. They're participating and taking ownership of their decisions. They're learning to plant, to weed, to harvest, to cook, and to preserve food for winter."

She looked straight at the judge. "This is what I do. This is my life. Helping people to make good choices about their food, and to equip them with lifelong skills."

Another judge leaned forward. "That sounds very noble, Miss Hiller. I'm sure these families appreciate your support. But you must be aware that the Miss Snowflake Pageant feeds into the Miss Tourism Montana Pageantry system, which goes on to Nationals and then to Internationals. What you're describing sounds good for Helena, but a needy family in Georgia isn't going to get any benefit from your good deeds here."

Marisa tipped her head to acknowledge his words. "There are other CSAs in this state, across the nation, and around the world. Most of them are independent and, to a large degree, I think that's a good thing. However, I'd love the opportunity to meet with their directors and talk about what they're doing with their less-than-perfect products. Is it going straight to compost, or are they sending it to food banks? Are local food banks equipped to handle perishable goods like freshly picked vegetables? Can other farms do what we've done, and help support local families in need through a shared-work program?"

She could see the gears turning in the judge's head.

"At Tomah CSA we're all about getting quality seasonal food into the kitchens of Helena's families. That's a goal easily expandable around the globe."

Another judge spoke up. "It's unusual to see such passion for needy children in someone as young as you are, Miss Hiller. Which came first, the passion for children, or joining the CSA?"

That one was easy. "The children. I've always had a soft spot for kids. Even here in Helena there are kids living on the streets." She remembered the youngster Jase had shared his lunch with. Could she find that child again? "As my career as a New York-based model grew, I became ever more aware of the wide gulf between the ultra-wealthy and those at the other end of the spectrum. My work took me to various countries in the third world, such as Kenya, where AIDS and drought have put millions of starving young children on city streets. When I returned to Helena, it was an easy choice for my mother and I to not only join the CSA but seek out ways to support those in need."

"Modeling and farming seem worlds apart," another judge mused. "Couldn't you have done more for the cause by remaining in your influential career than returning to Montana to get dirt under your fingernails?"

If only the woman knew the traumatic route that decision had taken. "It seemed the wisest decision at the time, and I don't regret a minute of it." Well, perhaps she regretted the venomous words she and Jase had stabbed at each other. But now that he was here and their relationship was on the mend, she couldn't hold onto the pain of the past. No, not when a bright future awaited — whether the tiara was won or lost.

"Your ancestor, Miss Calista Blythe, won the inaugural Miss Snowflake title in 1889, but turned it down to marry and provide a home for an abused orphan. You seem to have a lot in common with your ancestor. Can you see a situation where you might turn down the title for a perceived greater good?"

"Circumstances and culture are not the same one hundred and twenty five years later. Helena was a Wild West city with more wealth than it knew what to do with back then, and the rules of society were in a state of flux from old European standards to ways that meant something in the American West. Calista made the decision dictated by her society, her conscience, and her heart. Family history says she held no regrets."

"You didn't answer my question, Ms. Hiller. Would you ever come to a similar conclusion?"

What did the man mean, she hadn't answered? Hadn't

she said the West was a different place now, that society had changed to where such a decision would not be required? "Sir, if a situation arose that required me to choose between wearing the snowflake tiara and following my conscience, I would follow my conscience. No question. However, to the best of my knowledge, no such decision has been presented to me. I stand ready to represent the city of Helena to Montana and beyond."

Beyond might be putting it too strongly. How many years would she give pageantry? Like in Calista's day, she couldn't marry while in her reign — a stipulation that hadn't gone away in over a century. But who planned a wedding in under twelve months, anyway? Could she put it off longer than a year if she won the next round as well? *Would* she?

Her face flushed, and it wasn't just the heat from the spotlight. Jase hadn't asked her to marry him. Not yet. But that question couldn't be far away. What would she say? Would it matter to him if his fiancée spent an entire year traveling to draw attention to the needs of children?

That small boy in Last Chance Gulch drew her thoughts. No. He would understand. He'd even applaud.

"IT'S nice to have a couple of hours off from the pageant." Kristen kicked her shoes off and curled up in a deep leather chair across from Jase. "I'm glad Mrs. Jeffrey offered to keep the interviews on schedule this morning, but I hope I'm not missing anything I should be doing."

"You're doing exactly what you should be," Mom said

from the kitchen as Charlotte clambered up into Kristen's lap.

Jase tickled Liam's chubby tummy and the boy squealed. That little kid on Last Chance didn't have an extra ounce of fat on him anywhere. Why had it taken Jase so many years to start noticing needs around him?

Marisa's words haunted him. "What if I tell you my motives weren't completely pure?" So he'd been right back then. Sort of. Did it make a difference? But his hadn't been, either. He'd jumped to a conclusion and put all his self-righteousness behind his words. His lack of compassion boggled him now.

"Jase?" His mother's words filtered into his brain.

He looked up. "Pardon me?"

"I asked if you wanted to invite Marisa Hiller and her mother here for brunch Christmas morning. Maybe some of her friends. I'm finalizing numbers so I can send Nella for groceries."

What day was this, anyway? He checked his watch. The twenty-third? "Whose crazy idea was it to have a pageant the week before Christmas?" He pointed a finger at Kristen.

She shrugged. "We're following along the way the original pageant was done years ago. You're right, though. It's nuts."

"You didn't answer my question, Jase."

He took a deep breath. Was everything prepared? Would Marisa accept him? "I'll ask her, Mom. Don't know when I'll get the chance, though." He'd be so glad when this week was over and he could spend time with her without all this crazy pressure.

"When are you proposing, little brother?"

Jase's head flew up so fast he cracked his skull against Liam's chin. Luckily the kid was made of rubber and after a loud "oomph" ricocheted away to play with his trains.

"I... well, I don't know."

Mom hovered nearby. "But you're going to, aren't you? She seems like such a sweet girl." In a perfect world, his parents would get to know Marisa before he offered her a ring.

"Jase, can I give you some advice?"

He rolled his eyes at Kristen. "Since when have I been able to stop you?"

She chuckled as she stroked Charlotte's hair. "You have two choices. You can ask her in the next twenty-four hours and tell her it doesn't matter whether she wins or loses. Or you can wait for the results. Will she think you're offering her a consolation prize? Or that you're offering because of who she is as Miss Snowflake?"

He stared at Kristen. What did she know of his and Marisa's past? He wracked his brain. Nothing. He was sure of it. Unless Marisa had told her?

"If she thinks my love for her has anything to do with that tiara then we don't have grounds for a solid marriage."

"Look, I know something happened between you a few years ago." Kristen held up her hands. "I don't know the details, and I'm not asking for them. But I want you to know she's got my vote, and you need to think about the timing." She twirled her finger through Charlotte's hair.

Liam tackled him again from behind, nearly strangling Jase with his pudgy arms. Jase grabbed the tyke and hauled him upside down over the back of the chair, pinned Liam's arms together, and blew a raspberry on the little neck.

Yep. Jase knew it. He definitely wanted kids of his own. He yanked to his feet and dangled a writhing Liam by his ankles above Kristen. Charlotte pushed her brother, causing him to swing.

"I hear you." Jase lowered his nephew slowly to the floor and turned to his mother. "Sorry, Mom, but I can't stay for coffee. I've got a couple of errands to run before the stores close."

"But—"

"I'll let you know what she says as soon as I can."

Kristen giggled and Jase, hand on the doorknob, swung to face her. He couldn't keep the grin from poking the corners of his mouth.

"Let me know, too."

He waggled his eyebrows at her.

Now to find the perfect ring.

CHAPTER 16

*M*arisa fingered the valves on her flute as she waited in the wings for her name to be called, last of the ten semi-finalists. She hadn't played in public since high school band. She'd rarely even practiced since then. Not until Thanksgiving, when she'd made the decision to play *Away in a Manger* for her talent piece.

Dr. Mackie turned toward Marisa and announced her name to the sound of applause.

She strode onto the platform and set the yellowed sheets of music on the stand, then stepped beside it. It took several minutes for the crowd to settle down. That was a good sign, right?

After a smile and a wave, she raised the instrument to her lips. The beautiful words poured through her thoughts as she closed her eyes and joined her fingers with the Mueller version of the melody.

Bless all the dear children in Thy tender care.

God called people to be His hands and feet in caring for

the little ones. To show His heart. He'd called her, Marisa Hiller, to make a difference. Not just in Helena, but around the world.

Could she do that, even if it meant walking away from Jase Mackie? As the final notes of the sentimental carol hung in the electric silence of the banquet hall, she met his eyes.

Pride shone there, and love. Was the love strong enough? If not, this was the best time to find out. Maybe not today. It could wait until after the pageant, win or lose. But definitely before she fell even deeper into this mesmerizing dream.

She became aware of applause exploding through the room, of the judges furtively jotting notes at their table down front. She held Jase's gaze for a few seconds longer then reached for her music and headed offstage as Dr. Mackie entered from the other side.

A man in a black tuxedo offered glasses of water filled with clinking ice cubes to the other semi-finalists as Marisa stepped into the ready room. He turned toward her.

Mr. Penhaven? Who let him back here? Sure, they'd asked for volunteers, but wasn't this a bit much?

"Shh," one of the girls called. "Dr. Mackie is speaking."

The voice of the pageant director came through the speaker system. "I'm pleased to announce the five finalists for the Miss Snowflake Tiara. Miss Avalon Penhaven, representing the National Breast Cancer Coalition. Miss Diana Riley, representing the American Heart Association."

Marisa focused on the flute in her hands, ignoring Avalon's smug smile while Jase's dad added Heather and Tabitha to the list. Then, "Our fifth finalist is Miss Marisa Hiller, representing Tomah Community Supported Agriculture. Next we'll hear from each finalist while they share their particular platform. Each young lady will have two minutes to speak. Should the contestant continue past her allotted time, she will lose points."

She allowed herself to breathe. She didn't have to win. She wasn't even certain she wanted to. But the humiliation of losing to Avalon — ah, yes. That would be a sore spot for sure. At least she was in the top five.

Her attitude stank. Didn't the people counting on breast cancer research funds deserve a good shot at winning? Yeah, eating well would cut back on cancer in the nation. But still, it wasn't a popularity contest between herself and Avalon.

Jase had made it very clear he loved her, not Avalon. The prize of his love was worth far more than the tiara.

God's love was worth even more. She bowed her head. *Lord, grant me humility. Help me to be genuinely happy for the winner, whoever she is. Even if it's Avalon. It's not about me. It never has been. It's but about the message You've given me to share. I know it now, and I'll do the best I can. In Jesus' name, amen.*

"Marisa? That was a beautiful flute solo."

She jerked her head up and stared at Mr. Penhaven, inches from her face, as he held out the tray with glasses of water.

"Thank you." It didn't seem in character for him to be waiting on anyone, even his daughter, never mind being polite to Marisa.

Beyond him, Avalon smirked at her. There hadn't been a

single moment in the competition where Avalon had seemed friendly or even human. The real Avalon would be angry that her father said something nice to Marisa, yet the grin was all I-know-something-you-don't-know.

Hmm. Marisa looked sharply at Mr. Penhaven. "Why are you here?"

He shook his head and averted his gaze. "Perhaps this isn't the best time to speak of it."

"Speak of what?" She'd only met the man a few times before, in his office where they'd discussed her mutual funds. Surely that couldn't be his reason for coming to her during the competition — on Christmas Eve, no less?

"Well, I'm sorry, Marisa. I really am."

He didn't sound it. Her gut tightened.

"That portfolio we spoke of a few weeks ago has plummeted. I don't know what to tell you."

The savings for Davy and Lila's education. He was low enough to attempt to sideline Marisa during the competition. And Avalon's smirk showed she knew exactly what he'd attempt to do.

Applause came from the auditorium as Diana finished her speech.

Marisa lifted her chin and pierced Mr. Penhaven with her gaze. "I'll make an appointment to discuss it with you the first week of January."

"Welcome Miss Tomah CSA, Marisa Hiller."

Mr. Penhaven stepped aside as the audience clapped for her. A little smile toyed with his lips but did not reach his eyes.

Marisa took a deep breath and turned for the stage.

She wouldn't let him rattle her for her final appearance

before the judges. She couldn't afford to think about his bombshell.

JASE'S FINGERS itched to loosen his tie. The air in the auditorium seemed thick, but who could have more invested in this evening than the contestants did?

Than he did.

Yes, it mattered a great deal to him who won. Not that it changed his love for Marisa, but the next ten minutes would dictate what the next year of his life would look like. Filling his time with photography in Helena while he waited for her to fulfill her duties? Or maybe he'd be free to marry her sooner.

First he had to ask her.

Then she had to say yes.

She would, wouldn't she? A small green velvet box wedged in his tux pocket. She loved him. He knew it. They just had to admit it to each other.

His thoughts buzzed as Diana Riley answered stage questions from the judges. Marisa had drawn the second-to-last spot for the final segment of the evening. Only Avalon came after her. Avalon, with her smug, haughty smile all evening.

Jase cringed. He should have known better from the start. How could he have dated her even for a little while? Thank God he'd come to his senses before doing something foolish like proposing to the wrong woman.

His dad called Marisa's name and Jase held his breath.

Stunning in a hemlock green gown this evening, Marisa crossed the stage to the center.

Was it his imagination or did she look less self-assured than earlier? And why, when their eyes had been so completely locked as she played her flute, would she not even glance his direction now?

"You gave us a lovely rendition of *Away in a Manger* a few minutes ago, Miss Hiller," one of the judges said. "Please tell us how that particular song relates to your platform of—" He checked his notes. "Community Supported Agriculture."

Marisa closed her eyes for a brief instant and pulled herself together.

Could anyone else have noticed? Jase glanced around, but only expectation shone from faces in the crowd.

"One hundred and twenty-five years ago, my great-great-great grandmother Calista Blythe stood on a platform very like this one. *Away in a Manger* was a brand new carol then and spreading like wildfire around the world as people brought the simple words home to their hearts. Calista understood the deep longing for one small child to have a place to sleep that was warmer than a manger. Safer than a stable.

"In the days preceding the 1889 Miss Snowflake pageant, Calista harbored an orphan child, the indentured servant of a woman who abused her. A small child who had no place but a manger to lay her own sweet head, just like the little Lord Jesus.

"Calista laid everything on the line for this girl. She knew her actions could ruin her chance at winning the tiara and with it, the chance for enough funds to provide a home and family for the child."

Marisa's simple story held the audience enthralled.

From the corner of his eye, Jase saw Mr. Penhaven slide into his chair next to his wife and lean over to whisper something to her. She shook her head. The man shrugged and turned to face the stage, a sour look marring his face.

"My forebear understood the most important thing was not winning or losing a title or a tiara. It was knowing what God put her on earth to do, and doing it with all her heart."

Now Marisa looked straight at Jase. A challenge, maybe? "My passion for fresh, real food has been given me by God. There are many children in Montana, in the United States of America, and around the globe who do not have access to healthy food. Through my work with the Tomah CSA and its sister groups across our nation, I can make a difference. And when my time of wearing the tiara is complete, I'll continue to reach around the world in search of children in even more need."

She raised her chin slightly and looked from one judge to the next, taking a moment to make eye contact with each.

Jase's shirt buttons might not be able to hold his pride in her.

"I'll be honored to wear the snowflake tiara. But whether I win the tiara this evening or not, feeding hungry children in Helena or elsewhere is my life's focus." She met Jase's eyes. "The words of *Away in a Manger* spoke to Calista, and they speak to me. The song asks God to 'bless all the dear children in Thy tender care.' He wants me to do my part to bring that blessing in a practical way. And so I will."

She curtsied as the applause exploded. From over by the far door, Bren stood, weeping and clapping. Marisa's mom and Bob surged to their feet. Across the auditorium, people rose like a wave, applauding and cheering.

Jase watched her step back in line with the other top five finalists. It didn't matter if there weren't any photos of the next few minutes, did it?

CHAPTER 17

"W ell done, Marisa," whispered Kristen as Marisa passed her.

The applause from the auditorium continued for a long moment as they took a break to allow the judges' scores to be calculated.

Marisa squeezed her eyes shut. The guests in attendance hadn't clapped that long for any of the other girls, had they? How much did their approval matter to the judges? Parts of the scoring had been open to the community, but the results hadn't been released.

When she opened them again, Avalon stared at her through narrowed eyes from across the room.

Be near me, Lord Jesus, I ask Thee to stay close by me forever and love me, I pray. Bless all the dear children...

Avalon was a child in need of God's blessing. How could Marisa hold a grudge against her for wanting Jase's attention? She couldn't let that eat her soul any more, even if her opponent had hoped to cause Marisa to stumble after Mr. Penhaven's revelation.

The ready room door behind her creaked open and Avalon's eyes widened.

Marisa turned to see who had come in. Surely not Avalon's father again.

Jase.

From the platform, Dr. Mackie droned on, filling the time while the judges consulted with a running commentary of the week's highlights, but his voice disappeared.

Jase in a black tux, red hair under control for once. Tie on straight. Until his eyes caught her own and his fingers went for his collar.

Nothing existed. Kristen, Avalon, Diana, and the others drifted away along with Dr. Mackie's voice.

Jase stopped in front of her, caught both her hands in his, and tugged her aside. Not that a potted plant made much of a barricade. "Marisa," he whispered. "That was magnificent. You won the hearts of everyone here, all the judges."

He'd come all the way back to the ready room to tell her what the thunderous applause had already hinted at? He couldn't know more than she did. Not yet.

He cleared his throat. "You won *my* heart a long time ago on an African beach. Even though I said some hurtful things to you, I could never get you out of my thoughts. My hopes. My dreams."

Where was he going with this? In her heart, she knew. But why now? Why in the middle of the final moments of the Miss Snowflake pageant? Why with others nearby... his sister, Avalon?

"I love you, Marisa. I want you to know the outcome of

this evening doesn't affect that in any way. Whether you win or not, you will never be the runner-up for my love."

His hands clenched hers with a ferocity that was nearly painful. Or maybe she clung to him. Who knew?

But he dropped to one knee and let go of her right hand.

This was real. He was actually proposing right here. Right now.

A small box came out of the pocket of his tux and his blue-green eyes held hers firmly in their thrall. "Marisa, my love, will you marry me?" He popped open the velvet box.

Her voice caught in her throat. A cluster of diamonds in the shape of a snowflake glittered up at her. "Oh, Jase."

"Please say yes."

They had what it took to go the long haul, didn't they? Yes. Yes, they did. "Oh, Jase. Yes, I'll marry you."

He slid the diamond ring onto her finger then swept her into a hug and twirled her around, kissing her soundly.

"I hate to break this up, but Dad's calling for the finalists on stage."

Marisa caught her balance as Jase set her back on the floor, his hands still on her waist.

"I love you, Jase," she whispered, swooping in for one more little kiss even as she put her hands on his arms to push for her release.

Marisa tore her gaze from Jase's eyes and turned to the watching women. Kristen grinned, gave her a thumbs-up, and sent her to the back of the line.

Right behind Avalon, who looked like she would burst into tears any second now. Who could blame her? What could be worse than listening to your ex-boyfriend propose to your rival?

Marisa could only hope her hair and makeup weren't too mussed. But did it matter? Not anymore. Whether or not she won the title tonight, she'd gained something far more valuable.

A future with Jase.

THE TIARA GLEAMED on its velvet pedestal next to the microphone stand, with five floral bouquets arrayed around it. Jase picked up his camera and steadied his heart.

She'd said yes!

Right there on the stage, whether she wore the snowflake tiara or not, she wore the snowflake ring that bound them together. What more could he want?

Dad surveyed the group of finalists while Kristen waited off to the side. Then Dad made a show of opening the first envelope.

"Fourth runner-up is Miss ChildFund International, Miss Tabitha Jensen."

The audience clapped.

Jase took a deep breath. So far so good. He snapped a few photos while Kristen handed over one of the bouquets and gave Tabitha a smile and a few words Jase couldn't hear. Tabitha curtsied and waved to the audience.

"Third runner-up is Miss Habitat for Humanity, Miss Heather Francis."

More clapping, slightly more animated.

Snap, snap.

"Second runner-up is Miss National Breast Cancer Coalition, Miss Avalon Penhaven."

Jase dared a quick snatch for air. Avalon was so not going to be impressed. She'd done better than he expected, though. She smiled graciously at Kristen and accepted her bouquet before waving it in the air and stepping to the other side of Heather.

Down to two.

"First runner-up is…"

Dad paused and grinned, turning to Marisa and Diana. "…is Miss American Heart Association, Miss Diana Riley."

The room exploded.

Dad leaned into the microphone. "And the Snowflake Queen is Miss Tomah CSA, Miss Marisa Hiller."

At least, Dad's lips formed the shapes those words required. Jase could only hear snatches of them amid the crowd's uproar. But he couldn't have said anything else. Marisa was the last woman standing.

She'd done it. His professional training kicked in as he shot dozens of photos of Marisa. Accepting flowers from Kristen. Then a hug. And then the tiara.

Shaking hands with Dad, who leaned in and kissed her cheek.

A good sign.

Then she stood alone at the microphone. The Snowflake Queen. His beloved. His promised bride.

Marisa thanked the judges, thanked the sponsors and committee. She thanked the people of Helena. "My deepest gratitude goes to Bob Delaney, the chairman of Tomah Community Supported Agriculture, who encouraged me to enter this pageant on behalf of real food for everyone, whether they have a large grocery budget or not. Whether they live in Helena, in Montana, across these United States of America, or on faraway shores. I pledge to make the most of the favor you have bestowed on me and continue to promote healthy food however I can. Thank you."

She paused and leaned back into the mic. "Happy birthday to my beloved home state, Montana, and its capitol, Helena!"

The crowd roared its approval.

After snapping a few last shots, he hurried back to the ready room before Dad's closing speech. His sister awaited him, while the runners-up and the queen — queen of his heart — remained on stage a few moments longer.

Kristen catapulted into Jase's arms. "She did it! She did it! She won!"

He caught her somehow. Reflex, maybe, or self-preservation. He twirled Kristen around and set her back on the floor. It was hard to keep an eye on Marisa while spinning in circles with his sister.

"I'm sure you had a reason for your timing, little brother."

Jase didn't take his eyes off the platform. "Yep. You should know."

"But I never expected it right here, in front of everyone, in the middle of finals."

He spared her a glance. "It's been so busy I couldn't catch her alone. Trust me, I tried. This was my last chance."

"It took a lot of guts."

"You were right. I didn't want her ever to think I was offering either a reward or a consolation prize. She needed to know — right then, before the winner was announced, that she means everything to me." Man, his voice was choking up. "Whatever Dad said out there right after, it didn't matter. It doesn't affect us."

Kristen turned to face him fully. "It will take some getting used to, you being all grown up and a married man and all that. Wow, I can't wait to tell Todd and the kids. Charlotte and Liam love her already. Do Mom and Dad know?"

Jase grinned at his sister. "They knew it was coming, just not when." He nudged her as he pointed back at the stage. "Look at Dad."

Their father's eyes seemed riveted at something much lower than a woman's face, but rose when Marisa's left hand lifted to adjust her hair.

Kristen began to giggle. "He just saw the diamond ring."

Jase couldn't stop his smile from lifting both his ears. "Yep." He'd be doing a lot of smiling for a while, though the tiara resting on Marisa's hair meant their wedding was at least a full year off. They'd be busy the whole time. He could wait.

Dad took the microphone, thanked everyone for their support, and announced there would be a photo op on the stage in a few minutes for those who were close to the finalists.

The women turned and came toward the ready room, Marisa at the tail.

Jase held his breath, watching her beautiful, familiar face.

"Thanks a lot, buster."

He blinked as he reared back and focused on Avalon's stormy brown eyes. "Pardon me?"

She stood in front of him, hands on her hips. "Humiliating me in front of everyone by asking Marisa to marry you in public. And then she won. You probably rigged the votes."

"Miss Penhaven, please don't make accusations you'll later regret." Kristen stepped up beside them.

Avalon swung to face her. "Your whole family was in on this. It was never an impartial contest."

"It was totally fair. There was an entire board overseeing the pageant, and not a single one of the judges is related to the Mackie family. You heard the audience when Miss Hiller finished her final speech. When the announcement of the winner was made. Did Jase or I pay all those hundreds of people to pretend to be thrilled?"

Avalon scowled. "Your family has so much money you could afford to do it if you wanted."

Jase exchanged looks with Kristen. If Avalon thought it, no doubt her dad did, too. That was likely the reason for the studio rent increase.

Kristen's chin came up. "We didn't do it. You won't find a single shred of evidence. Not because we're so good at covering it up, but because it never happened."

Avalon's eyes filled with tears. "I wanted my dad to be proud of me," her voice little more than a whisper. "You don't understand. I needed to win."

Kristen put her hand on Avalon's arm. "Of course he's proud of you. Why wouldn't he be? You're an accomplished, beautiful woman."

But Jase knew it wasn't enough for Mr. Penhaven. "Avalon, I'm so thankful my parents love me and show their approval."

Kristen shot him a surprised glance, but he kept his focus on Avalon. "There's something far more important, though. People tend to react without thinking. Even parents. Even spouses." Even boyfriends. He didn't dare check where Marisa was, if she or the other women listened in. "We can't get our value from what other people think of us."

Avalon's brown eyes brimmed with tears, and one snaked down her cheek. She brushed it away.

"The only way we can get lasting value is from God. He created us. He declared us beautiful. Good. Made in His image. When we accept His love for us, it changes everything."

Kristen nodded. "What Jase says is true. It's like building a house on a sandy beach prone to tidal waves, versus building on a solid foundation. When we ground ourselves in God, it doesn't matter about the storms. We can still stand tall." She laughed. "Or you can, anyway. I'm too short to stand tall."

Avalon almost smiled. "Really? I've never thought much about God."

"Then it's a good time to start." Jase patted Avalon's arm. With any luck, that wouldn't propel her into his arms. "And you've created a lot of awareness for breast cancer, too. The foundation will be very pleased with all you've done."

"You think so?"

"I know so," Kristen answered firmly.

Avalon dashed away another stray tear. "I'm sorry. I just... I really counted on winning this."

With her eyes locked on his, Jase wasn't sure if she meant the tiara or him. Maybe both.

Aware that Marisa had slipped in beside him, he twined his fingers through hers and pulled her to his side.

Avalon's gaze lurched back and forth between them a few times. "Congratulations," she managed to get out before turning and hurrying away.

Jase slid his arm around Marisa and tugged her closer.

"You did a super job handling that," she whispered.

"I did?"

She leaned over and kissed him lightly. "You did."

Warmth spread through him as he turned her fully in his arms, his gaze catching on the tiara. "That snowflake looks good on you."

She grinned. "Which one?"

CHAPTER 18

She'd meant to pack up and sleep out at the farm Christmas Eve, but by the time the crowds thinned out and she and Jase had managed to say goodnight, it hardly seemed worth the effort. Diana had given her a congratulatory hug and driven back to Great Falls to have Christmas morning with her family, so Marisa'd had their room to herself for the little sleep she'd managed.

You ready? Jase texted.

Her bags were packed and stacked beside the bed. Marisa opened the door and walked into Jase's embrace.

She could so get used to this.

"Christmas Brunch is served, m'lady. Most of the guests have arrived. We're just waiting on the guest of honor."

"Do I need to wear the tiara?"

"Not today." He sobered. "You'll be wearing it a lot for the next twelve months. Enjoy the days off that you do have."

She ran her fingers down his clean-shaven jaw. "The wedding can't be for a year. It's in the rules."

"I know." He kissed her lightly then winked. "You up for a Christmas Day wedding next year?"

Marisa laughed. A whole year. It seemed so long, but would doubtless go quickly. "I don't think anyone would forgive us for messing with their holiday plans."

"You're probably right." He tapped his jaw. "The twenty-sixth?"

"How about early January?"

"You want me to wait an extra week or two?" Jase nuzzled her hair. "I'm not sure I can survive that long."

Marisa looped her hands around his neck and touched her forehead to his. "What are you going to do this year while you wait for me?"

He grinned. "Probably follow you around and take thousands of photos. Build a home for us here in Helena. That is, if you want to live here?"

They should probably have talked about these things before she agreed to marry him, but what did it matter? She'd go wherever he was and do it gladly. "If you want to."

"No, really." He rubbed his nose against hers. "You keep talking about Kenya. Do you want to go back there for our honeymoon? And afterward, I'd love to have the chance to do more documentaries about children in need."

Now that was a life calling she could get behind. "Helena would make a great home base for all that."

"It would, wouldn't it?" His lips claimed hers.

For twelve months, they'd only have stolen moments like this one. Even now, her future called them forward to the resort's dining hall. She pulled away reluctantly and tucked her arm through his as they strolled across the grounds. Snow sifted gently all around them.

The door swung open as they drew near. Christmas music and the aroma of cinnamon rolls spilled out.

"They're here!" called Jase's mom.

Did everyone in the room already know she and Jase were engaged? Marisa glanced around the guests. She'd told her mom last night, but Bob was here, and Bren and the kids, and others from the CSA, and a bunch of friends of the Mackies.

Jase slipped Marisa's coat from her shoulders. "I have an announcement to make."

When the guests quieted and turned toward them, Jase looked down at her with a smile. "I've asked Marisa to marry me, and she said yes!" He lifted their twined hands, exposing the diamond ring to scrutiny. "Save the date for the first Saturday in January, a year from now. You're all invited."

A cheer went up.

Bob cleared his throat. "While we're saving dates, how about Valentine's Day?"

Marisa stared at him then at her mother, grinning smugly at his side. What? When had this happened?

Bob winked at her. "I've asked Wendy to marry me, and we're too old to wait as long as these kids. So that's in six weeks, not a full year for us."

Marisa squealed and flung herself across the room into her mother's arms. "Really? I'm so happy for you."

Mom smoothed Marisa's hair. "Thanks, sweetie. I'm thrilled for you, too. I always wanted a son, and Jase will do just nicely."

And Marisa had always wanted a dad. Not sure Bob could fill that spot exactly, but she liked him well enough. He'd make Mom happy, and that was the main thing.

Wait. Bob had a farm. Mom had a farm... and Marisa wasn't going to be around to run it. She swiveled to catch Bren's eye.

Bren laughed. "I guess I have an announcement, too. I'm getting married..."

Everyone stared.

"Okay, I'm kidding about that. But Wendy has asked if I'd like to learn to manage Hiller Farm. I'm taking some courses through distance education and the kids and I will be moving out to the farmhouse at the end of January. I'm giving notice on our rental this week."

"Yay!" Marisa reached for her dear friend. How wonderful that her good fortune — and her mom's — could bring such a great result for Bren, Davy, and Lila. "Do I get to live there, too, in between all my trips?"

"You betcha. I'm counting on it. As if I'd dare kick you out of your own home! Besides, Baxter would never forgive me."

Two little girls sat half under the Christmas tree, hugging matching dollies.

"Kristen couldn't wait to give them their presents." Bren wiped tears from her eyes. "Thank you for letting me and the kids be part of your life."

"I wouldn't want it any other way." Marisa felt Jase's presence an instant before his arms slid around her from behind.

"Do you want to put your baby in the wooden cradle my daddy made?" Charlotte bent her head to peer at Lila.

"It's like the baby Jesus manger," Lila said in awe when

she caught a glimpse. She tucked her doll inside and rocked it. Both little girls began to sing *Away in a Manger*.

"Kristen got Lila a doll like Charlotte's?" Marisa whispered to Jase. "That's so sweet of her. Lila has had so little."

"My sister has her moments. But don't make too big a deal of it, or it'll go to her head."

"Oh, you." Kristen gave him a playful swat as she swept in with a hug for Marisa. "I'm delighted to be a part of what you're doing. Count on us." She waved a hand to encompass everyone in the room. "Not just to support for our Snowflake Queen, but to share your vision for Helena's families."

"And around the world," agreed Jase.

Marisa's heart filled to overflowing as Jase reclaimed her and kissed her, right there in front of everyone. She had the tiara, but, oh, so much more.

DEAR READER...

Thanks for reading *More Than a Tiara*! I'm so honored that you chose to spend the last few hours with Marisa, Jase, and me. You are appreciated.

Did the mentions of Marisa's ancestor, Calista, make you curious? If you love authentic fiction set in historical Montana, I'd love to introduce you to the writings of my friend Angela Breidenbach. Calista and Albert's romance is found in *The Debutante Queen*, first in Angela's Montana Beginnings series.

I'm an independent author who relies on my readers to help spread the word about stories you enjoy. Would you take a few minutes to let your friends know on Facebook, Instagram... wherever you hang out online? Also, each honest review at online retailers means a lot to me and helps other readers know if this is a book they might enjoy. I'd sure appreciate your help getting word out.

I welcome contact from readers. At my website, you can contact me via email, read my blog, and find me on social media. You can also sign up for my newsletter to be notified of new releases, contests, special deals, and more! You'll receive *Promise of Peppermint*, the ebook novella that introduces my Urban Farm Fresh Romance series absolutely free as my thank you gift!

Keep reading for a sneak peek of the next Christmas in Montana Romance, *Other Than a Halo*. I hope you'll join me in celebrating a love of Bren's own!

~ Valerie Comer
    www.valeriecomer.com
    http://valeriecomer.com/subscribe

OTHER THAN A
Halo

VALERIE COMER

OTHER THAN A HALO

CHAPTER 1

*D*on't you think it would be great fun for both girls?"

Bren Haddock stared at the mother of her daughter's best friend. "Um, no. I pretty much think you're crazy."

"What's crazy about it?" Kristen O'Brien's brown eyes lit up with excitement. "It's not competitive like the Miss Snowflake is for adult women. It's just for fun."

Bren spun her pottery mug on the table in Helena's Fire Tower Coffee Shop and raised her eyebrows. "Have you never heard of Crowns for Kids?"

"Of course I have." Kristen giggled. "Wasn't that *reality* —" she air-quoted the word "—show nuts? There was nothing real about it. And this won't be anything like it."

Bren had watched several episodes, aghast at what some people would do for fortune and fame. She shook her head. "I can't believe you want to put Lila and Charlotte through that. No way."

"Todd and I will gladly pay Lila's entrance fee and buy her dress—"

"No. I'm not a charity case."

Kristen's eyes softened. "I know that, Bren. I know how hard you've worked to get on your feet and make a solid home for your kids all on your own. How hard you work every single day. This is something Todd and I want to do. Call it our Christmas gift to Lila. She'll have a couple of adorable outfits and some happy memories of a perfect Christmas week spent with her bestest friend in the whole world." Kristen's voice mimicked Lila's.

"I don't see how it can lead to anything good." Bren met her friend's eyes across the wooden table. Around them, the lunch crowd drifted out. "I really don't. I appreciate that you guys have money and run in different circles than we do, but I don't want to get dragged into this. I don't want Lila thinking she can have whatever Charlotte has. She needs to learn to be satisfied with what I can provide, not want what other people have."

"I—"

"Being a single mom is hard, Kristen. I didn't even graduate from high school, thanks to being pregnant with Davy."

Kristen's hand touched Bren's arm. "I'm sorry you had to go through all that. I really am. I know you don't regret Davy and Lila, though."

"You're right. I love my kids, but look at me. I'm twenty-six with a nine-year-old and a seven-year-old. I finally got my GED and am taking college courses via correspondence. I'll be fifty before I get my degree at this rate. I want better for my kids."

"The pageant can help."

Bren shook her head. "Back to that, are we?"

"I'm serious. It will help teach both girls poise. Remind them there are hopes and dreams to reach for. And there are scholarships." Kristen leaned closer. "Besides, Marisa will coach them. You know how much they both adore her."

Who would ever have guessed that being one of the former model's projects would lead to all this? On a couple of underused acres and in her spare time — hard to believe her friend had any of that — Marisa and her mother had invited several single moms to grow food for their families.

Bren chose her words carefully. "Marisa is amazing. I can't thank her and Wendy enough for teaching me to cook and preserve food. I'm not the only person whose life she changed in more ways than one. She introduced me to Jesus." She chuckled. "But her year as Miss Snowflake isn't over until Christmas Eve, plus she's marrying your brother in January. How could she possibly have time to coach the girls?"

Also, why on earth were they still having this discussion? Did that mean Bren's resolve was weakening? Surely not.

"How about if their pageant dresses were their flower girl dresses?" Kristen's eyes sparkled. "How about if their talent was a song they could perform at the wedding?"

Bren sipped her now-cold coffee. One more try. She tilted her cup toward her friend. "Kristen. Look. I'm a black coffee kind of girl. No frills. I can't even remember what yours is called. I appreciate your friendship. I really do. But we're not in the same league."

"It's a sugar-free, white-chocolate mocha with a shot of peppermint and no whip." Kristen laughed. "And our taste in caffeine has nothing to do with life." Her gaze went past Bren's head. "Oooh. There's someone I want you to meet." She waved frantically then beckoned.

Bren turned slightly in her chair.

A tall guy with dark curly hair lifted his hand in response as he walked toward the front counter.

She swiveled back and glared at her friend. "Kristen. Don't even start."

"Start what?" Kristen winked. "He works for Todd at the ad agency. A Christian and new to Helena. What's not to like?"

The man placed his order at the counter, giving Bren the chance to look him over. Those curls brushed the collar of a tailored suede jacket that ended at narrow hips. He glanced over his shoulder and met her gaze. A small smile played at the corners of his mouth.

Bren snapped her gaze back to Kristen.

"Cute, isn't he?" whispered her friend. Her traitorous friend.

"Looks that way." Bren kept her voice even. "I really should get going. I have to—"

"School isn't out for another hour. You don't have to be anywhere."

"Kristen."

"Hmm?"

"Stop trying to set me up. I'm not looking for a man, okay?" Even good-looking guys could be jerks. She should know.

"It's not like tha—" Kristen glanced over her shoulder. "Oh, hi, Rob. Care to join us?"

He towered over the table, a mug in his hand. "Hello,

Kristen. Nice to see you. I don't believe I've met your friend." His dark eyes looked Bren over.

Bren's lips tightened into a hard line.

"Rob, this is Bren Haddock. She's the single mom of Charlotte's best friend, Lila."

Way to slide in the single part.

"Bren, this is Rob Santoro. He recently moved here from... Spokane, wasn't it, Rob?"

He nodded as he flipped a chair around and straddled it. "Via Billings. But yes, I'm Spokane born and bred. Most of my extended family still lives there, all within about six blocks of each other."

"But you escaped to Montana." Kristen giggled.

Rob's grin was lopsided. "Someone had to. Big families have their place, but I got tired of everyone being in my business all the time."

"I wouldn't know." Kristen sighed. "When my parents bought Grizzly Gulch Resort a few years ago and my little brother moved here to open his photography studio, it didn't take Todd and me long to decide Helena trumped Salt Lake City. We love being near family."

"My father has four brothers. I have fifteen cousins. They all live in Spokane. Every last one of them except for a couple who escaped for college. They'll be back."

Bren could only imagine. Much as she craved a sense of family, Rob's did sound a bit overwhelming.

"How about you?" Rob turned to Bren. "Do you come from a big family?"

"No." No need to tell a guy she just met that her parents' bitter divorce had estranged her from both of them. "It's just me and my kids."

Kristen placed her hand on Bren's arm. "My parents have all but adopted them, though. And the church has, too. Everyone needs family."

It was hard to let down her guard. Bren had been on her own for so long it still seemed hard to believe she'd found any sort of security. One of these days the rug would get pulled from under her, and she'd be on her own again. Granted, she had more skills than before and a bit of savings now, but where could a high school dropout whose job experience was farm operation find another job? Marisa and her mom both said Bren could keep managing and living on Hiller Farm, but someday that would change.

"Todd says your specialty is marketing for events. Bren and I were just talking about the Miss Snowflake pageant for the little girls. Todd says you'll be the one handling that?"

Rob glanced at Bren, questions in his eyes.

She raised her chin. So she didn't look the part of a pageant mom. What did it matter? She'd turned Kristen down. What this guy thought of her didn't make a speck of difference.

WHY DID that seem like a loaded question? Kristen looked innocent enough, but Rob had been to the O'Brien house for dinner a couple of times, and he knew she had a quick wit with complex thought processes. He'd bet anything she was matchmaking, but what man wanted a ready-made family? Not him. Still, he wouldn't be rude. Couldn't be.

"Yes, Todd asked me to handle that portfolio." He smiled at Bren. She was pretty in an earthy way, with wavy blond hair pulled into a long ponytail. He turned back to Kristen. "If you have any ideas for the marketing campaign, I'm all ears. I'll admit I've never done a promo for a pageant before, and I'm still debating what angle to take with it."

"There are two stages. I think. The first is awareness and getting people to sign their daughters up for it. And then, once we have a full complement, marketing to get viewers interested. That part will be easier because the events will be in tandem with this year's Miss Snowflake events."

Bren shifted in her seat and glanced at her watch.

Kristen touched Bren's arm. "Don't rush off. You still have plenty of time before Lila and Davy's bus."

Bren pushed back her chair and glared at her friend. "I'm not sure why I'm in this discussion, as we won't be taking part. I can catch up with you later."

"Bren. Please."

"Kristen. No."

Rob looked from one to the other. Interesting. Todd had laughed, saying his wife was a force to be reckoned with. The evidence was in front of him as she stared down her friend, not giving an inch.

Bren sighed. "This conversation is over, Kristen. I don't see any need to parade Lila around in makeup, slinky clothes, and overdone hair, pretending to be on a manhunt. She's seven. Just a little kid who should be allowed to be one."

"What part of *this is not Crowns for Kids* did you miss? It's a no-glitz pageant. I don't want Charlotte acting seventeen either."

"It's the gateway drug. Don't you see?"

Rob checked his own watch. Did he really need to listen to them hash it out?

Kristen turned to him. "This is where the first stage of marketing comes in. Many of the parents will be just like Bren: concerned about pressuring their little girls to grow up too quickly."

Bren crossed her arms. "This is a bad thing how?"

"Of course," Kristen went on, "there will also be little divas signed up who already demand their wishes on a silver platter. That can't be helped, but we will stand firm and create a family-friendly atmosphere."

Rob was beginning to see the challenge. Bren had fire in her eyes. No pushover, this one. She likely had to be strong to raise her kids alone. "Bren, I'm interested in what your objections are. You mentioned not wanting your daughter to grow up too quickly. Can you fill me in on some of the other issues you see?"

Kristen hid her smirk behind her coffee cup.

Bren glared at her friend before turning to Rob. "That's the big one, but money is another." She held up a hand as Kristen opened her mouth to speak. "I don't know how much it costs, but just the fact that Kristen offered to pay for it tells me it's outside my budget. There's clothes she'd need, coaching, hair and makeup—"

"I told you. No glitz."

Rob pulled out a notebook and began scribbling.

"—driving her to practices and events. Keeping family life balanced with Davy. And most of all, raising her hopes that she'll win and then her being crushed. Fairy tale meets crash ending right at Christmas. Talk about timing."

He finished his shorthand notes and glanced up. "Anything else?"

She leveled him a stare. "I think that about covers it."

Rob chewed on the end of his pen. "Maybe her dad would be willing to help with expenses." Although what if Bren were widowed, not divorced? Had he put his foot in it?

Her chair scraped on the wooden floor as she surged to her feet. She set both hands on the table and leaned in on him. "Maybe he's in jail for dealing drugs. Maybe he's out again. I've lost track. He's never been interested in Lila, and I'm certainly not going to remind him. I'd prefer he kept on forgetting."

Bren's brown eyes glittered in her almost elfin face. Rob felt himself staring, caught up in her firestorm.

"I *am* leaving now. Nice to meet you, Rob. I'll deal with you later, Kristen." She grabbed a bright green oversized purse held together with buckles and strode toward the door, skinny jeans tucked into calf-length boots.

Kristen giggled. "Well, I think that went over rather well."

The door jingled shut. Bren's brown jacket crossed the window then disappeared.

Rob forced his gaze back to his boss's still chuckling wife. Kristen might not be wrong.

Other Than a Halo
is available in paperback
wherever you purchased
More Than a Tiara!

ABOUT VALERIE COMER

Valerie Comer's life on a small farm in western Canada provides the seed for stories of contemporary Christian romance. Like many of her characters, Valerie grows much of her own food and is active in the local foods movement as well as her church. She only hopes her imaginary friends enjoy their happily-ever-afters as much as she does hers, shared with her husband, adult kids, and adorable grand-daughters.

Valerie is a *USA Today* bestselling author and a two-time Word Award winner. She writes engaging characters, strong communities, and deep faith into her green clean romances.

To find out more, visit her website at www.valeriecomer.com, where you can read her blog, explore her many links, and sign up for her monthly email newsletter, where you will find news, giveaways, deals, book recommendations and more. You can also find Valerie blogging with other authors of Christian contemporary romance at Inspy Romance.

Made in the USA
Monee, IL
27 September 2021